Gideon is in an odd position. He's the first human ambassador to the Ogorth clan, and while he loves his new job, he could do without the war brewing. He's not ready to lose his new friends or the alliance he and the dragons have been working so hard to establish.

And he's not ready to lose Lisha, the beautiful healer who saved his life when he was poisoned.

Lisha can't stay away from Gideon, even though he probably should. He has no idea how to deal with a human, and with the Saganto clan attacking so many small clans, he's overworked and having a hard time dealing with what he sees.

The Saganto clan won't stop until they destroy the Ogorth clan and anyone who's allied with them, but once the Ogorth clan discovers when the Saganto clan plans to attack, they might have a chance to win.

But it won't be easy.

Bronze Victory
Copyright © 2023 Catherine Lievens
ISBN: 978-1-4874-3997-2
Cover art by Angela Waters

Published by eXtasy Books Inc

Look for us online at:
www.eXtasybooks.com

Bronze Victory
Ogorth 8

By

Catherine Lievens

CHAPTER ONE

Lisha made his way down the hallway. Luckily for him and every other healer in the palace, the infirmary was pretty empty right now. That meant he had time to check up on his other patients, including the egg Christian had found in the forest.

He didn't really need to. He'd already checked the egg, and it was perfect. Whoever had hidden it had done a good job and protected the egg. Lisha couldn't help but wonder what had happened to its parents. No one would abandon an egg like that. If someone didn't want the child after laying an egg, the clan would have taken care of it. There would have been no need to abandon the egg, especially in a place where they couldn't be sure it would be found.

So why leave it there? What would have happened if Christian hadn't stumbled onto it?

Lisha shuddered at the thought. The egg would have eventually hatched, and the baby would have been alone. It would have been near impossible for them to survive, and while Lisha worried that the egg's parents had tried coming back for it and couldn't find it, Christian had done the only thing anyone could have done. He couldn't have left the egg where it was. It would have been too dangerous.

That was why Lisha thought the parents must have left the egg there because they hadn't had a choice. The Ogorth clan always gave its members a choice, especially about something like this, so Lisha suspected the parents came from another clan.

It was a possibility. So many small clans were disappearing with every attack from the Saganto clan. That clan was killing as many dragons as they could, but some were bound to manage to get away, and once they did, they were on the run. If they couldn't find a safe place to hide or a new clan, they were on their own, which was dangerous, especially with the Saganto clan still attacking left and right.

Lisha wished there was more he could do, but beyond taking care of any survivor who managed to reach the Ogorth clan, he was helpless. His job was nowhere near as important as the queen's, and he was glad. He wouldn't know where to start if he were in her place — or on her throne.

At least the egg was safe. For now, Christian was taking care of it, even though his partner, Ruy, was wary because he didn't want children any time soon. The fact that they didn't know who the egg belonged to made the situation even more complicated, but Christian was human. He didn't care about the different clans. He just cared that the egg had been abandoned and needed someone to take care of it. He probably felt responsible. since he'd been the one to find it.

Hopefully, they'd find where the egg had come from. Even if its parents couldn't care for it, it could return to its own clan. Until that happened, though, the egg was a member of the Ogorth clan, and Lisha would take care of it.

When he reached Christian's door, he knocked. Christian was living with Ruy, but during the day, when Ruy was at work, he spent most of his time with his human family. That was where Lisha knew to find him, so he'd expected Christian to be the one to open the door.

Christian grinned as if he was happy to see Lisha.

Lisha was slightly puzzled because, as far as he was aware, they weren't friends, even though they were friendly.

"Are you here to check on Humpty Dumpty?" Christian asked.

Lisha frowned. "I'm sorry?"

"The egg."

"Yes. I'm here for the egg."

Christian stepped aside to let Lisha in. "It's fine. Nothing has changed as far as I can see. No cracks or anything."

"That's because it's not yet ready to hatch."

Christian bobbed his head. "I know, but I'm impatient. I can't even imagine what it's like for the parents. Humans just come out of their mother, and they're here."

Whereas dragon eggs were laid, then needed more time for the dragon inside the egg to be ready to come into the world. It was the only way Lisha had known for most of his life, but he could understand why Christian was excited and impatient. The dragon world was new to him, and while he'd adapted, it couldn't be easy. Everything was different here, and Lisha was impressed at how much Christian already looked at home.

Christian guided him toward the couch. Things were changing in the castle, and it was partly because of the humans who now lived here. Before them, most of the clan had spent their time in their dragon form. Even when they were in their human form, it was easier for them to use the furniture they used in their dragon form. Lisha was used to wide, comfortable nests, but this room was set up for the family of humans who lived here. There was no nest in sight. Instead, there was a table with several chairs, and in a corner in front of a TV, couches, armchairs, and a coffee table. The TV was on, showing colorful cartoons.

And on the couch, surrounded by pillows as if Christian was afraid it would topple over, was the egg.

Lisha looked from the egg to the TV. "You do realize the baby is unable to watch this, right?"

Christian rubbed the back of his neck. "I know. It's just weird to treat it like an object when I know there's a baby in there."

Lisha supposed that was better than Christian treating it like it didn't matter. Even though the egg wasn't his, he behaved like it was, and it warmed Lisha's heart.

He was glad Christian had gotten over his crush on him. Lisha had been aware of it, especially after Christian had asked him out. He liked Christian, but not like that, and besides, Christian was perfect with Ruy.

He sat on the couch and gently collected the egg from its nest of pillows. Christian hovered by as he waited, and it was clear he really was worried about the egg. He wanted the baby inside of it to be okay, like everyone else. Those two belonged together.

Lisha took his time. He always did when it came to eggs and young dragons, because it was better to take more time to examine them than to miss something. Luckily, the egg was perfectly healthy, and when Lisha held it toward the light, he could see the faint outline of the dragon inside of it. It was growing quickly, but it would still take some time for the baby to be ready to hatch. It was small, but everything looked the way it should.

That was what Lisha told Christian when he was done. He settled the egg back against the pillows and got up, but he should have known he wouldn't be able to leave easily. Like most humans who now lived with the clan, Christian was chatty.

"You look tired," he said.

Lisha blinked. "I actually have less work than usual at the moment."

"Then you should use that free time to sleep."

Lisha looked out the window. He probably should, but he was worried and had a bad feeling. The queen had sent groups of guards into the forest to look for the egg's parents. Part of Lisha hoped they wouldn't find anyone, because that might mean they'd made it out alive. If they found anyone at this point, they'd probably be in bad shape. No one had noticed unknown dragons hunting in the forest, which meant that the egg's parents had to be starving, and that was if they hadn't been wounded when they'd reached the Ogorth clan.

"I'm worried, too," Christian said as he looked outside the same window as Lisha. "Have you heard anything?"

"No, but if there's someone out there, the guards will find them."

The problem was that no one could tell what state they would be in when that happened.

It was taking everything Gideon had not to start screaming and bouncing on his feet. He didn't know how else someone should react when they were packing to move in with the dragon clan in their freaking palace.

It was a serious situation. Gideon wasn't moving in with the dragons to have fun or because he wanted to. He did want to move there, but he had a job to do, and he took that very seriously.

He was the first human ambassador to the Ogorth clan.

The possibilities this role opened were mind-boggling. It wasn't even only about the Ogorth clan. The dragon world was a bit of a mess right now, with one clan trying to take over the others, but Gideon was confident they'd eventually be defeated. *That* was when the fun would start. It was when things would settle down, and hopefully, once they had, dragons and humans would be able to live in harmony.

He snorted as he pushed a shoe into his suitcase. That sounded like a utopia. He didn't think harmony could exist, not between humans and dragons, not within the human race, and not within the dragon race. It seemed the dragons were more similar to humans than anyone had thought. There were bad ones, and there were good ones, just like human beings. Unfortunately, that meant there was little chance for harmony.

But peace, they could probably manage.

Gideon's phone vibrated on his nightstand. He already knew who it was and was tempted not to answer, but his mother would freak out if he didn't. She was already worried enough about everything that was happening, and he didn't want her to wonder if she was ever going to see him alive again.

Of course she would. He was moving to another job, not the cemetery.

"Hey, Mom," he said as he answered.

"I hope I didn't catch you at a bad moment."

"I'm packing."

She clicked her tongue. "I still wish you hadn't taken this job."

Gideon was very much aware of that because she'd already told him several times. "I wouldn't have said no even if I wanted to, and I didn't. This is an incredible opportunity, Mom. I'm an *ambassador*." Yes, it was because the queen had requested he be the one to fill the role, but that meant he'd made a good impression on her, even though he wasn't sure he had what it took to do the job.

"And I'm happy for you. I realize how big of a promotion this is, but I worry. If only this job could be in another country rather than with those dragons."

Gideon didn't blame his mother. She hadn't been to the palace, and she hadn't met the clan. She'd never even met a dragon, for that matter. If Gideon were going to another country, he'd have to deal with human beings, and she knew humans, but she didn't know dragons beyond what she saw on TV and the little Gideon had told her. She didn't know what to think of them, and no matter how many times Gideon reassured her that he'd be all right, he was moving far away, and for the first time in their lives, she wouldn't be able to reach him easily.

It was a big change for all of them, and while she was anxious, Gideon was more excited than he could remember ever being.

"I promise I'll be all right," he said as he sat on the edge of the mattress.

His bedroom was a mess. He was permanently moving into the palace, and it was a logistical nightmare. He couldn't bring most of his stuff, including the furniture. He'd been selling it piece by piece, and what he couldn't get rid of, he was planning on gifting. A lot of the rest would end up in a storage unit. Maybe in time, he'd be able to retrieve some of it.

But for now, he wanted to focus on his future, not on his past. He was only taking the bare minimum, but once he was settled, he could have things shipped out to him.

"I know you've said that, but they're *dragons*," Gideon's mother whispered.

"And just like humans, there are good and bad dragons. The Ogorth clan is on the right side, I promise. They welcomed me when I was there."

Someone had also poisoned Gideon while he was there, but he wasn't about to tell his mother. She didn't know about it and would never find out if he had his way.

He didn't blame the Ogorth clan for what had happened to him. They hadn't been involved in the poisoning, and they'd taken care of him when they'd realized what had happened. Gideon didn't think he would ever forget waking up in bed, feeling like shit, and seeing an angel sitting beside him.

Well, not an angel. Lisha was a dragon shifter, but he was beautiful like an angel. He'd taken care of Gideon while Gideon recuperated, and Gideon had been sorry to leave him behind.

When he thought about Lisha, his heart beat faster. He had a bit of a crush on the healer. Normally, he wouldn't have dwelled on that feeling, but he was moving in with the clan. That meant he'd have many opportunities to see and talk to Lisha.

He almost squealed. He was so fucking excited.

"You're probably right," Gideon's mother admitted. "You know them better than I do. I just don't like that you'll be so far away from me."

"Phones exist, Mom. Just use yours and call me whenever you want. I'll try to answer, but don't freak out if I don't. I'm not going there on vacation."

"I know. This is your job, and I'm proud of you. I need to stop treating you like a child. You're an adult, and I trust that you know what you're doing."

Gideon had been an adult for a while now since he was in his mid-thirties, but he didn't point that out. He understood where his mother was coming from and didn't blame her. Her worry wasn't going to stop him from doing this, though.

It was a big promotion, but more importantly, it meant that Gideon was moving in with the dragons. He'd always been fascinated by them, even when he thought they were animals. Now that he knew they weren't and that they could turn into humans, or at the very least, that they had something that resembled a human form, he was even more excited. He could discover so many things and get to know so many new people he wouldn't have known otherwise. How was he supposed to be afraid?

He didn't even care that someone had poisoned him. He trusted the Ogorth clan with his life and knew he wouldn't regret it. The only thing he was worried about was that a war was brewing, and he'd find himself right in the middle of it, but that was something he would deal with when he had to, and not one second sooner.

For a while, he wanted to ignore the alarm bells in his mind. He wanted to focus on how happy he was about this new job and all the things he would learn.

He also wanted to make a difference. He'd been horrified for so long at the treatment of dragons. Even if they'd been animals, the way they were hunted hadn't been right. Gideon had been an activist in his youth but hadn't succeeded.

But now, he had the chance to make a real difference, and he wasn't letting it go. He was the first human ambassador to the Ogorth clan, and he took that role very seriously, especially with the war brewing. He was convinced that dragons and humans could survive and thrive together.

And he was going to show everyone that he was right.

CHAPTER TWO

The palace was buzzing. There was no other word to describe the tension and gossip. Lisha usually didn't care much about gossip, but he couldn't have avoided knowing what was happening.

The humans were coming back.

That in itself wasn't new for the Ogorth clan. Ever since Orran had returned with a human in tow from his mission to retrieve the queen's egg from the person who'd stolen it, humans had been making themselves at home at the palace. First, it had been Blake, then his brother Sheldon. Others had followed, and now the small group of humans was an integral part of the clan. They had children with clan dragons, and they were effectively clan members.

Lisha didn't have anything against that. He'd talked to the humans many times, and he liked them. He'd also taken care of their children when they were still in their egg and when they'd hatched, and he could see that their fathers were good additions to the clan. The fact that they were humans didn't matter. He wasn't like the older dragons, who were wary and didn't want humans to change the clan.

They didn't realize that the clan was already changing, and it wasn't because of the humans. It was because of the greed of another clan, or rather, of its leader.

There had been peace between the dragon clans for a long time, but that peace was over, and it wasn't the fault of the humans who lived with the Ogorth clan or even the clan's fault. It was what it was, and they needed to deal with what was being handed to them.

Besides, more humans wanted to help. That was why a group of them, including Gideon, was moving into the palace.

Lisha looked out the window. He didn't know when the human would arrive, and Lisha didn't understand how he could have so readily agreed to move here. Wasn't he afraid he would be poisoned again or hurt another way? The queen had made sure that the person who'd poisoned Gideon paid for it, but they belonged to another clan. Maybe that was why Gideon was coming back. Maybe he trusted the Ogorth clan.

Lisha did, but not everything was well. The Ogorth clan had many members, and not all of them were good people. He just had to look at what had happened to some of his friends to have proof of that. Still, as much as some clan dragons disliked humans and didn't want Gideon to be here, they wanted the Saganto clan to take over even less. That meant following the queen's orders even when they disagreed with her. It meant accepting that the human government was going to help.

Unfortunately, it didn't give the clan an advantage, because the Saganto clan worked with hunters. The thought made Lisha shudder, and he tried to focus on the cleaning he was doing in the infirmary, but the task couldn't hold his attention. He didn't have to think to scrub counters.

Hunters had been a problem for dragons for as long as there had been humans and dragons. They hunted dragons, sold their eggs and their children, and tore their bodies to pieces to sell them. It was horrifying and one of the reasons the dragon clans were so isolated. They were stronger than humans, but there were so many more humans than dragons that if there was an uprising, the humans would take out the clans. That was one of the reasons it was so important to have a good alliance in place with humans. No one wanted a war between humans and dragons. It was bad enough that there was a war between dragon clans.

"I've heard he's pretty," Atha, one of Lisha's colleagues said from where she was sitting nearby.

A small group of nurses and healers had gathered at the other side of the infirmary. They were peeking out the window, waiting for the humans to appear. They would arrive in the air, carried by dragons. It was the only way to get to the palace, even though there were small doors at the mountain's base. The forest around the palace was too thick to allow any vehicle to reach them, which was good. It made it slightly awkward when they were moving a bunch of humans in, though.

"You'll have to ask Lisha," Neena, another healer, said. "He took care of him when he was hurt. I didn't see him at his best, but he was cute."

Lisha almost rolled his eyes. "I'm not going to talk about Gideon with any of you."

The two dragons laughed. "Gideon, huh?"

Lisha told himself he didn't have anything to be embarrassed about. "It's his name, as I'm sure you know."

"We do. We also want to know if he's pretty."

Lisha tried not to think of Gideon, but it was impossible. Gideon *was* pretty. He looked nothing like what Lisha was used to, since he wasn't a dragon, but that didn't take away any of his appeal.

He was shorter than Lisha, but most humans were shorter than dragons. The last time Lisha had seen him, his short brown hair had been messy because he'd been spending a lot of time in bed recuperating. There had been dark shadows around his warm brown eyes, but he'd been upbeat and acting as if he hadn't been poisoned.

Gideon wasn't handsome like some of the men Lisha had seen on the Internet. He was skinny and not very muscled, and his nose was slightly too big for his face. His smile and the way he looked at the world made up for it. He wore glasses, and Lisha loved that he'd kept pushing up the frames. It probably meant the glasses were too big for his face, but it was endearing to see.

No, Gideon might not be the most handsome man Lisha had ever seen, but that didn't mean Lisha didn't like him or that he wasn't pretty.

"I think someone has a crush," Atha said with a giggle.

Lisha rolled his eyes. "I don't have a crush."

"Well, maybe you don't, but everyone knows that Gideon does."

Lisha's stomach churned even though it shouldn't. "Does he? Who does he like?"

"You," Neena quickly said. "I didn't spend a lot of time with him, but it was obvious."

Lisha told himself not to hope. What did it matter if Gideon had a crush on him? He didn't have a crush on Gideon.

Or at least, that was what he was trying to convince himself.

Flying was an experience Gideon wanted to repeat. He'd gotten to do it to come and go from the palace the last time he'd been here, but it was always exhilarating. Every time, Gideon felt like he could touch the sky with just a finger, and technically, he supposed he could. He and the others had been flown in through the clouds, and while Gideon was pretty sure he'd heard Jennifer shriek several times, he'd loved it.

He wasn't sure what his three guards thought of it. He'd complained that he was required to take them along, but his boss hadn't taken no for an answer. The man was unhappy that Gideon only had four people with him. He probably thought the dragons would eat him, and while Gideon hadn't pointed out that a guard or two wouldn't stop them if it was

13

what they wanted, he'd thought it.

No one in the Ogorth clan would try to eat him. He didn't need Nate, Jacob, and Edgar. He could watch his own back. Besides, no one here would hurt him.

They finally landed, and as soon as Gideon was off the back of the dragon he'd been riding, she shifted back. He grinned at her, and while she looked puzzled, she smiled back.

"Thank you for giving me a ride," he told her, lightly bowing.

She blinked. "I followed orders."

"I realize that, but I enjoyed myself very much."

"Start taking their things down to their rooms," a strong voice declared.

Gideon grinned as he turned to Slavin. He'd met the dragon when he'd been here the last time, and they'd become friends. "It's good to see you again."

Slavin grinned back. "Glad to see you made it here in one piece. Morven wanted to be present, but he's with the queen."

"That's fine. I don't need him to show me around the palace again. I already know where everything is."

"You're staying in the same room as last time," Slavin confirmed. "And you'll see Morven soon enough. He and the queen want to see you in about half an hour."

If Gideon had things his way, he'd head to the throne room right now. His team was frazzled, though, and Jennifer looked like she might be about to faint. The three guards were masking their feelings better, but he could tell they were nervous. None of them had been here the last time Gideon had visited. They'd volunteered to move with him, but he suspected it had more to do with the paycheck than anything else. It wasn't a problem. Either they'd learn to live with dragons, or they'd resign and move back home.

"Let me take you to your rooms," Slavin said with a smile as he turned to the other three.

To Gideon's surprise, Jennifer stepped forward. "My name is Jennifer, and I'm Gideon's assistant. It's a pleasure to meet you."

"I'm Slavin. I work closely with the queen and her right-hand man, Morven. If you need anything, feel free to contact me." He looked at Gideon. "We left a list of important numbers in everyone's room. You already have mine, of course."

Gideon tried not to beam like an idiot. He didn't want to look creepy, but he was so freaking happy to be back.

It was odd. Until recently, he hadn't known dragons could become humans. He'd felt a kind of kinship with dragons, but that was because of all the work he'd done to protect them when he was younger. Here at the palace, he felt more at home than he ever had anywhere else. It didn't make sense, because he was human, but he couldn't deny that was how he felt. He could see himself growing old here. It wouldn't happen anytime soon since he was only in his mid-thirties, but he had every intention of retiring here.

That meant he needed to make sure the palace was still standing by the time this stupid war was over.

He and the other four followed Slavin from the landing pad into the palace. He still got a lot of stares, but most of the dragons had seen him when he'd been here before. Several even waved at him, and he waved back, feeling like a child in his excitement. Surely, starting a new job shouldn't feel like this.

"I'll be back in half an hour," Slavin promised once they reached the rooms that were now theirs.

They were all in the same hallway, so they'd be able to find each other easily. It also meant the guards that were supposed to keep Gideon safe would be able to reach him in any circumstance.

"None of you need to come with me when I meet the queen," he told them.

He should have known better. Jacob glared at him while Jennifer quickly opened her purse to take out her phone.

"I'm supposed to take notes when you have meetings," she said.

"I know, but this won't be an official meeting. The queen wants to welcome me back."

"The fact that you talk about her as if she's a friend is, well, I don't know what it is, so I'll do my best to ignore it at the moment," Jennifer said. "We're here to work."

"I'm aware of that, but that's not the only reason for our presence. This is our new home. You just arrived, so I'm sure you want to explore and find out where everything is. The palace is marvelous, and most of the people who live here are friendly. I don't need any of you to come with me, because I'm safe here. You don't have to worry."

Jacob crossed his arms over his chest. "Where you're going, I'm going."

Gideon wouldn't win, so he nodded. He might as well not fight Jacob because the man was more stubborn than he was.

Half an hour later, Gideon had showered and changed. He'd done his best to smooth down his hair and thought he looked presentable enough to meet the queen.

As promised, Slavin came back to pick up him and his Jacob-shaped shadow. He didn't say anything about Jacob's presence, for which Gideon was grateful. He didn't like the thought of needing a guard and didn't think he did. It was the only way this was going to happen, though. His superior had been clear that he was an ambassador now, which meant he had to follow the protocols.

"She's eager to see you again," Slavin said.

"The same goes for me. I love the palace and your queen." He really did. She was a great person and a good queen, and while working with her was intimidating, Gideon couldn't wait to get started.

But they didn't work during this meeting. When Gideon got to the throne room, he found out that Ita had organized to have something to eat and drink so they could relax. Gideon was glad, because he was starving, and while he was still a bit awkward in the queen's presence, he'd get over it eventually. It was easier to relax when everything felt less official than it was.

"It's a pleasure to have you back with us," Ita told Gideon.

Something in her tone told Gideon that she was telling the truth. "And it's a pleasure to be back. I don't know how to thank you for allowing me to move in with your clan. I'll work as hard as I can to keep everyone safe."

A quick knock on the door made both of them turn. One of the doors opened, and a dragon rushed in. They barely looked at Gideon before bowing to the queen. "The guards came back."

Ita sat up on her throne. "And they found something?"

"A body. They found a body."

Lisha was working in the infirmary when the door flew open. He expected the worst, and he wasn't wrong. He knew something had happened from the look on the guard's face.

"What is it?" he asked, turning away from the pregnant dragon he'd been examining.

She was too nauseous to keep food down, so he'd been watching her through her pregnancy. She'd be fine, and she only had a few weeks to go before the egg was ready to be laid.

The guard stared for a second as if they didn't know what to say. Their eyes were wide, and they were pale, maybe from shock. They appeared to be young, so it was possible that whatever had happened was the first time they were confronted by something shocking.

Lisha left the pregnant dragon on the bed and waved at Atha to take care of her while he went to stand in front of the guard and snapped his fingers. The guard jolted back, then finally seemed to get over his shock.

"We found a body in the forest."

Lisha briefly closed his eyes and sighed. He'd known there was only a slim chance they'd find the egg's parents alive. He'd hoped anyway, but not anymore. "Where is it?"

"Still at the ground level, in an empty room. We weren't sure if we should bring them here."

"No. I'll go there. Does the queen know?"

"Someone was sent to tell her."

Lisha nodded and looked around the room. He could do this on his own, but he might need help. He didn't want to force anyone, but the people who worked with him were used to blood and death. He was relieved when Neena stepped forward without hesitation. She didn't waste time reaching for Lisha's bag and checking that he had everything he needed.

He took it from her, hauled it on his shoulder, and gestured at the guard to lead the way.

They were silent on their way downstairs, and the tension was heavy. Everyone was worried, even though, as far as Lisha knew, no one from the clan was missing. The body had to belong to one of the egg's parents, but he wouldn't be sure until he saw it, and there was always a possibility that a clan member had perished.

They went lower and lower, taking corridors that were crowded first, then mostly empty. Most clan members stayed in the upper part of the castle and never used the doors on the lower levels. They were human-sized, and the dragons preferred to fly. Lisha did, too.

He felt like he was about to throw up by the time the guard stopped in front of an open door. They cleared their throat and knocked but didn't move to step inside, instead moving away so Lisha could. Lisha swallowed and told himself that this would be over soon, and hopefully, he'd have some answers.

The room was well-illuminated. There was no furniture inside except for a long table that had been covered in plastic. On it was a body covered by a white sheet. Morven stood next to the table, his hands behind his back, looking grim.

Lisha hesitated for a moment. He knew what to do, but it was never easy. He sucked in a breath, then straightened his back and strode toward the table. "Do we know anything?"

"Not much. The body was found curled up at the bottom of a tree. There are signs they weren't alone, but we didn't find anyone else. This dragon wasn't a clan member."

Lisha nodded. His hands trembled when he reached for the sheet, but his movements smoothed out as he revealed the body under it.

The dragon had been a beautiful green. The color was more muted now because they were dead and had been for a while, but they would have been gorgeous alive. Lisha tried not to think of them in that circumstance and focused on doing his job. He dropped the sheet at the feet of the body and turned to open his bag. Once he had gloves on, he went to work.

"This dragon recently laid an egg," he said out loud. "I can't give you a time frame, but I'd say a few weeks. The color matches the egg Christian found, so while I can't be a hundred percent sure, I think I can say this is one of the egg's parents."

"Anything else?"

"They were wounded." Lisha poked at the deep bite in the dragon's thigh. "They lost a lot of blood, but they survived long enough that it got infected. It wasn't a quick or easy death."

It made Lisha angry. This dragon should have lived long enough to see their egg hatch and to meet their child. They should have been safe and would have been if the Saganto clan wasn't tearing through the dragon world. Lisha didn't know what had happened exactly, but this dragon had been attacked while they were heavily pregnant. What kind of monster would do that?

He knew what kind. The kind who fought with the Saganto clan. The kind who killed dragons who wanted nothing more than to live in peace, have precious children and build families.

Lisha's eyes prickled, but he swallowed and fought the urge to cry. "I don't know where this dragon came from, but I think they initially survived an attack. They were bitten on the thigh, so I'd be surprised if they managed to reach our forest on their own. They have to have had someone with them to help them walk."

"They didn't die alone?"

Lisha prayed they hadn't. "I can't tell you that."

"But you can take a guess."

Lisha looked up. Morven looked as shitty as Lisha felt. "If I had to guess, I hope they didn't. I hope they escaped with the egg's other parent so whoever was after them would follow rather than turn their attention to the egg. I don't know what happened to the other parent." Lisha hoped they'd find them, but what would be the odds that they'd be alive?

Morven nodded. "I'll take a picture and ask Sheldon to contact the clans we've allied with. Maybe someone will recognize them."

It would be their only chance to identify the dragon, but it was a slim one. The Saganto clan had destroyed many smaller clans, leaving no survivors. If this dragon had come from one of those, there might not be anyone left alive who could recognize them.

But there was nothing else they could do. They still didn't know who the dragon was or where they'd come from. They might never find out.

Lisha had never felt so powerless.

CHAPTER THREE

Lisha didn't need to see the egg again. He'd examined it a few days ago, and while he wanted to keep an eye on it, nothing would have changed in such a short time. There was no reason for him to be knocking on Christian's door, yet here he was.

He knew why he was here. He felt responsible for the egg, especially now that he knew that one of the egg's parents was gone. Christian was tasked with keeping the egg safe, but Lisha needed to reassure himself that the egg was fine. The baby inside had lost one of their parents, and the second parent probably wouldn't come back, and Lisha wished he could have done more for the baby.

At least Christian had found the egg. Lisha didn't even want to think about what would have happened if the egg had hatched in the forest. The baby would have been on their own, and they probably would have died, just like their parents. Here, they would be fine. The egg would never be alone, even if they never found any remaining family members. If Christian couldn't adopt them, someone in the Ogorth clan would, and the baby would be safe.

The door swung open. Christian's expression turned grim when he saw Lisha, and he stepped aside right away as if he understood why Lisha was here. Knowing him, he probably did. He was a sensitive man, and like everyone in the clan, he'd heard about the body. No matter how hard someone tried to keep something a secret in the clan, it never worked for long. Lisha hadn't talked about the body, but he wasn't surprised that the news had gone around like wildfire.

"The egg is fine," Christian said in a gentle voice. "It's on the couch."

This time, the TV was off. Christian's phone was on the couch next to the egg, so he'd probably been sitting next to it. He was taking his role as a temporary parent very seriously, making Lisha like him a little more.

Not that Lisha needed to like him any more than he already did. He didn't want to date Christian, so he was glad Christian had found Ruy, but he liked the human. Christian was a nice person, and Lisha could see them being friends. He didn't care that Christian was human, just like Christian didn't care that he wasn't.

The egg wasn't the only thing in the living room area. Gideon stood there, his eyes wide as he stared at Lisha. Lisha hadn't expected him, and he wasn't quite sure how to react.

Things had been odd between them before Gideon had left. They'd grown close while Lisha kept an eye on Gideon after he'd been poisoned, and Lisha liked him, but they'd both known Gideon needed to leave. They'd also both known he'd come back, but Lisha hadn't expected Gideon to look for him when he did, and he'd been right. Gideon had been busy with the queen and everything else, and Lisha didn't hold that against him. Besides, they'd been friendly, but in the end, Lisha was nothing more than the healer who had helped Gideon when he needed it.

But now, Gideon was staring at Lisha with stars in his eyes, and it made Lisha feel self-conscious. He had no idea how to behave or what to say, but he was here for the egg, so he could focus on that. He didn't want to be rude, though. Gideon was an ambassador, which meant that he wasn't going anywhere. He was effectively a clan member, and Lisha needed to learn to live with him.

"It's good to see you," Lisha said.

Gideon's glasses slid down his nose, and he quickly

pushed them up. "It's good to see you, too," he said. "I'm sorry. I didn't know the egg had a doctor's visit."

"It doesn't. Well, it didn't. I was just anxious and wanted to check in."

Gideon's smile faded a bit. "I understand."

"Do you?"

"I was there when the queen was told about the body. She didn't give me details, but it's impossible not to hear gossip. They were the egg's parent?"

Lisha looked at the egg. It was sitting completely still in the middle of a nest of pillows. There were no cracks, which was good, but it wouldn't last forever. Lisha could protect the egg, but protecting a baby dragon would be more complicated. Besides, babies needed parents. They needed people who loved them. Would they be able to give the egg that?

"That's what we think," he confirmed. "There were signs, but of course, we can't be a hundred percent sure."

"I'm really sorry for all of this."

"It's not your fault."

Gideon smiled gently. "It might not be, but it doesn't mean I don't have empathy. It's good to know that the egg will be safe and protected. I'm sorry its parents are gone, but the baby will have a good life anyway."

He was right. Lisha kept telling himself this, but after examining the body, it was harder. Even though he knew the egg would be safe and the baby would thrive with the clan, the baby still had lost a lot, and so had their parents. It wasn't fair. Nothing the Saganto clan was doing was fair.

Lisha crouched in front of the egg and gently touched it. He stroked his palm down its length, testing the strength of the shell. The entire time, he could feel Gideon's gaze on him. Gideon was clearly fascinated, which, considering humans didn't lay eggs, was understandable.

"I didn't expect to find you here," Lisha said.

Gideon chuckled and rubbed a hand on the back of his neck. "I was visiting with Christian."

"That, and you're obsessed with eggs," Christian said, his tone making it clear that he was teasing.

"Not obsessed," Gideon protested. "It's just so different, and the egg is beautiful."

It was, but then, eggs were always beautiful. The promise they held, the future they implied, all of it was important to the clan and to dragons. Dragons weren't fertile often. Even when they were fertile, they didn't always choose to have a child. When they did, they considered the child precious, as it should be.

That was why it hurt so much. Lisha could imagine how the egg's parents had felt. They'd wanted to create a new life, to expand their family, and they had. They'd had their entire future in front of them, and they'd been planning for it.

But instead of living that future, one of the parents was dead, and the other was probably gone. The egg was safe, but the baby inside of it would never know their parents, and a special kind of sorrow came with that knowledge.

"You're a good person, Gideon," Lisha blurted out.

Gideon blinked at him. "Thank you. I try."

Lisha was pretty sure that Gideon would be a good person even if he didn't try. It was just who he was.

It would have been easy for him to accuse the Ogorth clan of trying to kill him and to ruin the alliance between the clan and the humans, but he hadn't. He'd been poisoned, yet he hadn't had any worries for his own safety. He hadn't blamed the Ogorth clan for what had happened and never would. He was working hard to support the alliance, had never treated dragons any differently than he treated the humans Lisha had seen him with, and generally looked at home at the palace. It was surprising, although maybe it shouldn't have been. Lisha had seen how easily some humans adapted, and Gideon was one of those humans. More than that, he was enthusiastic about living with dragons and getting to know them in a way that was a little overwhelming sometimes.

But all of that came from a good place and a good heart. That was what fascinated Lisha the most. He'd never been interested in having a lengthy relationship with anyone in the clan, but Gideon?

That was an entirely different situation.

Gideon couldn't look away from Lisha and the egg. He wasn't sure which one fascinated him the most, and he wasn't sure it mattered, either.

Knowing that a baby was inside that egg, growing and getting ready to come out, was wonderful. It was a bit like a human pregnancy, and even though Gideon wasn't involved in any of this, he wanted to keep the egg safe. It contained an innocent child who'd lost their parents, and while Gideon knew that the Ogorth clan would keep the baby safe, he couldn't help it.

He'd always been overprotective. When he was a child, he'd brought home stray kittens and puppies and, on one occasion, a wounded mouse. After that stunt, his mother hadn't been happy with him, but Gideon couldn't have abandoned the mouse on the side of the road to die. He didn't care that it was a mouse. It had been hurt, and Gideon had wanted to help.

He felt the same way now, but this wasn't his fight. The egg wasn't hurt. In fact, it was safe, and it always would be. The Ogorth clan would make sure of that. Gideon wasn't responsible for the egg, and he had nothing to do with the situation.

He was still involved. The Ogorth clan was his new home. He didn't know if the egg would stay here, but Gideon wanted to help while it did.

Watching Lisha check the egg was something Gideon couldn't look away from. Lisha's movements were smooth and practiced as he turned the egg this way and that. When he raised it to the light, Gideon sucked in a breath. He couldn't see inside the egg from where he was, but he knew that was what Lisha was doing.

It got Lisha's attention, and the healer turned to look at him. "Do you want to see?"

He didn't have to ask twice. Gideon scrambled to go stand behind Lisha. He peeked at the egg, delighted when he could see the outline of a tiny wing.

The baby was in their dragon form. That was how it always was, or so he'd been told. The fact that they could turn into humans after birth was fascinating and incredible, but then Gideon started to realize that everything was fascinating and incredible here.

It was entirely new to him, but it was so good.

"Can you tell if it's a boy or girl?" he asked.

Lisha wrinkled his nose. "Why do humans always ask that?"

Gideon knew that Lisha had some experience with human parents. Several of the humans who lived at the palace had had children with their dragon partners, and Lisha would have been the one to deal with them. There were other healers at the palace, but most of the humans were in relationships with dragons close to the queen, and from what Gideon had gathered, Lisha was the queen's personal healer. She would have wanted him to take care of those babies, especially since they were human and dragon hybrids.

"I guess we're curious," Gideon explained. "Some humans prefer to have one over the other, but not all. It also helps to know how to decorate the baby's room and stuff."

Lisha frowned. "The baby's room? Why aren't they with

their parents? Why do they have their own room?"

"Where do the young dragons sleep?"

"In the nest with their parent."

Lisha made it sound like it was natural, and it probably was. "I'm pretty sure baby dragons are sturdier than human babies. Babies aren't supposed to be in bed with their parents. It can be dangerous."

Lisha frowned. "So I should tell parents that?"

"Well, you know them better than I do, and you've been doing this for a while. Human doctors tell parents not to sleep in bed with their children, though. Of course, those children can't turn into dragons, so there's that."

Lisha nodded, but he was frowning and possibly still thinking about what Gideon had just said. The differences between them and their cultures was something Gideon wanted to explore, but not right now. Right now, he wanted to explore Lisha more, and the thought made him blush.

Lisha noticed it. He put the egg back into the nest of pillows, then turned to Gideon. "Are you feeling all right?"

"I'm fine."

"Are you sure? You look flustered."

That was because Gideon *was* flustered. Even when he'd been stuck in bed after being poisoned, he hadn't been able to look away from Lisha. The healer had spent a lot of time with him, probably because the clan was terrified that Gideon would freak out and accuse them of poisoning him. Lisha had been keeping an eye on him, and they'd talked a lot.

Lisha was a gentle soul but also incredibly strong. He cared for the clan and didn't discriminate between humans, dragons, or dragon hybrids. He'd welcomed Gideon with open arms and had done everything he could to make sure he was healthy.

And he was beautiful.

Lisha looked nothing like a human, but that didn't mean

there wasn't beauty in him. When they were in the same room, Gideon couldn't look away. He was fascinated by the way the light played on Lisha's bronze skin. It was a metallic color, but Gideon knew that if he touched it, it would be soft and warm. The scaly patches would feel different, but that was one of the reasons Gideon wanted to touch them — to feel the contrast between softness and sturdiness, between human and dragon. His fingers itched with the need, so he pushed his hands into his pockets, just in case.

He liked Lisha, and he was pretty sure Lisha liked him, at least as a friend. Gideon was here to do his job as the new ambassador, but he was also here to build a life. He wasn't going anywhere as long as the alliance between the clan and the human government stood. This was his home now. If he wanted a relationship and a family, he'd have to build them with a dragon shifter.

That was perfectly fine with him, especially if the dragon shifter was Lisha.

There was no way for Gideon to know if Lisha felt the same way. He'd taken care of him, but that was because it was his job as a healer. He hadn't reached out to Gideon since Gideon had moved back into the palace, but then, he was probably busy, and Gideon had been, too. Gideon would never find out if Lisha liked him if he didn't ask. It was terrifying, but a lot of things in Gideon's recent life had been.

Lisha turned back to Christian, who'd been silent throughout the visit. His gaze bounced from Gideon to Lisha, and Gideon knew he was in trouble when his friend beamed. Christian was going to want to talk about this, and Gideon had no idea what to tell him.

"Everything is fine," Lisha said as he moved toward the door. "I'm sorry I bothered you."

Christian shook his head. "It wasn't a bother. I think we all worry about the egg and the baby inside of it." His gaze flickered to Gideon again. "Gideon was just leaving. Maybe the two of you could walk out together? I have to use the bathroom."

Lisha blinked as if he didn't understand why Christian was telling him that, and maybe he didn't. He couldn't see that Christian was trying to push them together, but Gideon could, and he was torn between wanting to thank his friend and wanting to strangle him.

Maybe he should see how things went before he made that decision.

Lisha waited for Gideon at the door. Gideon quickly stroked the egg one last time, waved at Christian, then followed the healer. It was almost as if Christian couldn't wait for them to leave, because the door slammed closed only seconds later. Lisha and Gideon looked at each other, then Lisha gestured down the hallway.

"Where are you headed?"

"I should probably go to my office."

"You have work to do?"

"Doesn't everyone?" But Gideon wasn't ready to let Lisha go. The problem was that he didn't know how to keep him with him.

Gideon was right. Lisha had work to do, patients to see, and many other things to focus on, but there was a problem.

He couldn't stop thinking about Gideon.

Gideon was adorably flustered. He was an adult, so Lisha probably shouldn't be thinking about him as adorable, but he couldn't help it. No matter how old Gideon was, there was something refreshingly candid about him. He wasn't naïve or stupid—he wouldn't be an ambassador to the Ogorth clan if he were—but he seemed to take everything in stride and to have a positive outlook on life. Lisha didn't always manage to do that, and spending time with Gideon made him smile and believe that everything truly would be all right. It might only be an impression, but it felt good and made Lisha feel lighter.

"I'll walk you back to the infirmary," Gideon declared.

Their time together was coming to an end, and Lisha didn't like that. Saying yes to Gideon's offer meant having him around for a bit longer, and Lisha couldn't find it in himself to say no.

Gideon talked a lot. Lisha had noticed that the first time Gideon had visited the clan, and it was impossible to ignore now. As they walked, Gideon kept up a mostly one-sided conversation that made Lisha smile. He was entertaining, and since Lisha didn't enjoy talking a lot, it fit both of them.

He couldn't help but wonder what Gideon thought of him. He'd seen the way Gideon watched him, but he was afraid to hope. And truly want him? He was a dragon shifter, not a human. The humans who lived with the clan didn't seem to have a problem with the fact that their partners were dragons, but their situation was different. They were clan members. They didn't have links to the human government or anything like that. They weren't here to work.

But Gideon was. Lisha wasn't quite sure what being an ambassador meant, but it was a role that would keep him here for a long time, possibly years. Would Gideon want to be alone the entire time? Would he take lovers he wouldn't care much about? Or would he look for a relationship? If he did, what would happen if his government called him back?

Lisha had many questions, and he wasn't sure if he should ask them. He didn't want to make Gideon uncomfortable, and maybe he didn't want to know if Gideon wouldn't be here forever. He needed to be careful, and it would be wise for him to stay away from Gideon, but he didn't think he could. Gideon brought the sun into Lisha's life. He made him smile more than anyone ever had, and he didn't seem to expect anything from him. He wasn't perfect by any means, but neither was Lisha. Did it matter that their situation was complicated? Complicated didn't mean they couldn't work things out.

Gideon had never once acted as if he was afraid or disgusted by dragons or by the thought of dragons being with humans. He was friends with Christian, who was dating a dragon shifter. He'd been spending time with the other humans in the clan, and most of them were in love with dragons.

"Anyway, I didn't tell my family about the poison thing," Gideon said, catching Lisha's attention.

"Why?"

"They would have worried too much. I mean, I'm fine, aren't I? You took care of me, and I'm as good as new. I didn't want to freak out my mother by telling her about it when it was already over."

"But she'd want to know."

"I know. I also know she would have tried to make me change my mind about accepting this job if I'd told her." Gideon hesitated. "She doesn't know any dragon shifters. She only knows what I've told her about you and your people, and even though I've had only good things to say, she's still wary. I don't blame her, but I can too easily imagine her reaction if I told her I'd been poisoned. No, it's better this way. She's already worried because I moved here with the clan. She doesn't need to worry that I'm going to die, too."

"How are you feeling?"

Gideon laughed. "Not like I'm going to die. I'm perfectly fine, Lisha. You took care of me, and I'll always be grateful. I'm pretty sure you saved my life."

Lisha looked away, feeling flustered. "I did what any healer would have done."

"Probably. That doesn't change the fact that you saved my life, and I'll always be grateful for that."

Lisha hadn't been in many relationships. He'd always been too busy, first studying and apprenticing, then being a healer. He had no idea how to seduce Gideon or even what to tell him. Thankfully, they were interrupted. Orran was coming toward them down the hallway, and he smiled as he reached them.

"Gideon, Lisha," he said, nodding at both of them.

Lisha nodded back. "Orran." He turned to Gideon. "If you'll excuse me, I have to go back to the infirmary."

Gideon frowned for a moment, then smiled again. "Of course. I kept you away from your work long enough. I can still walk you there."

"I'll be fine. I'm sure you and Orran have something to talk about." It felt like Gideon had something to talk about with every clan member, which was amusing and endearing.

Gideon's eyes lit up. "You're right."

"Then I'll leave you to it. I'll see you soon," he promised.

He quickly nodded at Orran again, then turned to walk down the hallway. He could feel Gideon still watching him, but he didn't turn around. He wasn't sure he'd have been able to leave if he had.

He didn't know what it was about Gideon, but he wanted to spend his entire day with the human. It was probably nothing more than a crush, but he'd had crushes before, and they hadn't felt this consuming and like they could be life-changing.

That was one more thing that frightened Lisha. He could too easily see himself falling in love with Gideon, but what would happen if he did?

Gideon couldn't help it. He watched Lisha walk away until he turned the corner, and Gideon couldn't see him anymore. Only then did he turn his attention to Orran, who was staring at him.

"Sorry about that," Gideon told him, hoping he wasn't blushing.

"You like him," Orran said simply.

Gideon's first instinct was to deny it, but why should he? If he had his way, he'd live with the Ogorth clan until he died, and Lisha would be by his side. He didn't have time to focus on a relationship with Lisha at the moment, but eventually things would calm down, and when they did, Gideon had every intention of seducing Lisha and convincing him to spend the rest of his life with him.

He shrugged. "I do. He's a fascinating person, and he's beautiful."

"He is."

Gideon narrowed his eyes. "Did you have a relationship with him or something?"

Orran laughed. "No, I never had a relationship with Lisha. It doesn't mean he's not a friend, though."

Gideon needed to stop embarrassing himself. "Right. Sorry."

"You have nothing to be sorry about. It's good to see that you're interested in Lisha. Many people are worried about him."

"Why? Is something wrong with him?"

"Not as far as I know. He's always worked a lot, though, which is understandable. He's not just a healer. He's the queen's personal healer, and that comes with a lot of prestige but also a lot of work. He's been overdoing it lately. He feels responsible for the egg, especially now that one of its parents has been found dead. He also knows there's a war coming and that he'll have to take care of the wounded. We've been welcoming as many refugees as we can, which isn't nearly enough, and it's been hard on everyone, but the healers especially."

Everything Orran was saying made sense. Gideon wanted to take some of the burden off Lisha's shoulders, but he didn't know if he could or if there was anything else he could do to help. He wasn't a healer by any means, and he couldn't take care of anyone. He could barely take care of himself. Sometimes he bought a few plants, and he always ended up killing them. His mother teased him that he got them to bring home to die, and she wasn't wrong.

But he wanted to take care of Lisha. He wanted to make him feel safe and protected, to be the rock in Lisha's life when there was a storm, to be the person Lisha came back to every night. He wasn't sure he was capable of doing all of that, but he was certainly willing to try.

"I can't say I expected you and Lisha to end up together, but I like it," Orran said.

Gideon wondered if he'd missed part of the conversation. He wasn't about to ask, because he was too interested in what Orran was saying. "We're not in a relationship."

"Yet."

Gideon bit his lower lip. "And would it be a problem if we were?"

"You're asking if me or my friends would have a problem with you and Lisha being together because you're human and he's not?"

Considering Orran lived with a human, Gideon understood why he thought it was a stupid question. "It's more that I work for the government, and a lot of you don't trust humans. I don't blame you."

"I wouldn't blame you for not trusting dragons after you were poisoned. To answer your question, I don't have any problems with you and Lisha being together. In fact, I quite like the idea. Lisha takes care of everyone and needs someone to take care of him. I think you could be that person."

Gideon nodded. "I like taking care of people." He always

had. He loved making people feel cherished and giving them everything they could ever want. It wasn't always possible, but it didn't mean he wasn't going to try, especially when it came to Lisha.

"He works too much and too hard," Orran said as he looked out the window. "That's not going to get better for a while. The Saganto clan is set on destroying us, and they're taking down as many dragons as they can. Hopefully, we'll be able to stop them, but many people will be hurt even if we do. Lisha will feel responsible for all of them. He's focused on his work, which means he doesn't have a lot of friends or time away from work. My friends and I have been trying to get him to open up and spend more time away from the infirmary now that he has the opportunity to do so, but it's not always easy." He grinned at Gideon. "I think that having you around would be an incentive."

"I'll take care of him," Gideon promised. He'd already been planning on doing so anyway.

"I know you will. It's good to have you back with us and to know that you won't be leaving anytime soon."

Gideon didn't have many friends. He was awkward and had a hard time trusting people. Between that, getting older, and working a lot, he barely had anyone in his life. Moving in with the clan wouldn't fix all of it, but getting to know Orran and the others made him feel like maybe, in time, he could start trusting more people and welcome them into his life. It wasn't just Lisha, either.

The move with the clan had given Gideon a lot more than he'd expected and could have hoped for. It was also giving him war and the very real possibility that he might get hurt — or worse — but that wasn't something he wanted to dwell on. No matter what happened with the Saganto clan, Gideon wasn't going anywhere.

And he'd prove that to Lisha.

CHAPTER FOUR

"The Kanada clan is gone."

Lisha stared at Neena, trying to make sense of the words. "What happened?" He knew what had happened. He didn't have to ask but needed to hear it anyway.

She looked away. Her jaw was tight, and her expression grim. "The Saganto clan."

"Are there any survivors?"

"I don't know."

Lisha could go to the queen and ask her, but he wasn't sure it was a good idea. Did he really want the queen to tell him that no one had survived? That was how things usually went when the Saganto clan attacked. They didn't leave anyone behind. They burned down the home of the clan they attacked, killed every dragon, and stole their eggs and babies. Lisha's stomach churned at the thought that this could have happened to the egg Christian was taking care of. It had happened to many others, and knowing what the Saganto clan was doing horrified him. Unfortunately, there was nothing he could do. He wasn't a fighter, but even if he had been, he was only one dragon. What could he or anyone else do against the Saganto clan?

Lisha couldn't help any of these people, but he could help his own. He needed to focus on his clan and do what he could for them, but it wasn't always easy. Everyone wanted to talk about what was happening. They wanted to be reassured, but no one could do that for them. There were no reassurances. There was only the knowledge that the Saganto clan would eventually come for them.

Lisha wasn't sure they'd be ready to face them when it happened.

He wanted to believe the Ogorth clan would be strong enough to defeat them, but he wasn't sure that was the case. The Saganto clan showed how strong they were by destroying other clans, even though they were smaller. So far, they hadn't attacked bigger clans, but they were going to eventually.

Their final goal was to take down the Ogorth clan. Their leader had taken it personally when the queen had agreed to an alliance with humans. She'd tried convincing other leaders that it was the only way the dragon race could survive, and some clans agreed with her. The Saganto clan hadn't and had allied with hunters—humans—which was hypocritical of them, but they weren't doing this to keep their people safe. They were doing it because they wanted revenge on the Ogorth clan and to take over the world. At least, that was what Lisha had heard.

It was ridiculous. They were dragons, not gods. They might be stronger than humans, but it didn't give them the right to kill humans and take over their lives. It seemed the Saganto clan was planning to turn the humans into slaves or kill all of them. Lisha wasn't sure how they thought that would work, but he didn't see how it could.

That wouldn't stop them from trying.

He swallowed. "I'll go ask Morven if he knows something," he told Neena.

"It's fine. I don't think anyone knows what's going on, and it'll be too dangerous to send help right now."

"We need to know more." What if there were people out there who needed Lisha's help?

"I don't think there are any survivors, Lisha. We'd already know if there were, right?"

Probably. If there was anything the clan was good at, it was getting gossip and news around as fast as lightning. Lisha would probably know everything about the attack in an hour, from when it started to how long the fire had burned.

He hated that.

No one had told him anything yet, and while he was anxious, he wasn't sure he wanted to know more. Neena was right. He didn't need to ask to know what had happened. It wouldn't be the first time the Saganto clan completely destroyed another clan. They'd been doing so for weeks, and they were getting closer.

But not being able to do anything wasn't something Lisha was used to. He didn't want to stay here, sitting in the infirmary, thinking about what was happening with his hands in his lap. Surely, there was something he could do. He was ready to help with anything at this point, even if it didn't have anything to do with healing.

But his place was here, in the palace with the Ogorth clan, healing Ogorth clan members and following the queen's orders. She'd call for him if she needed him, but she hadn't.

For now.

Neena got up to make some tea, and Lisha looked out the infirmary's window. The view of the forest was one he knew well. He'd been watching it since he'd started working, and he couldn't imagine a life in which he wasn't a healer. His stomach churned as he thought of what would happen if the Saganto clan took over. Unfortunately, it was too easy to imagine.

They would kill everyone — the queen, for sure, along with the people who worked more closely with her, like Morven and Slavin. They'd kill her son, too, and probably all the dragon-human hybrids. They'd definitely kill the humans.

They might keep Lisha and the other healers alive because they could be useful, but anyone who might rebel against them would be gone. All of Lisha's friends and Gideon would die. There was nothing Lisha would be able to do about it because he couldn't fight his way out of a wet paper bag.

But that wasn't something he could fix, either. He was a healer, and his job was to care for wounded and ill people, people in pain. He couldn't create that pain, and he didn't know if he could defend himself even if he was forced to.

He prayed he would never find out, but he knew he would. A war was coming, and no one would be able to avoid it, not even him.

Everyone in the palace was worried. Gideon hadn't understood why until he'd found out about the new clan that the Saganto clan had destroyed. Then he'd become worried, too, but there was nothing he could do.

Technically, what was happening was none of his business. He was here as an ambassador between humans and dragons and shouldn't be directly involved in the war between the dragon clans. But the main reason he'd been appointed ambassador was to help the Ogorth clan fight the Saganto clan, and he took that seriously.

He didn't know the Saganto clan well, but considering what they were doing, there was no way that their winning the war between clans would be a good thing for anyone, even humans. That was what he'd told his boss when they'd talked earlier, and he was convinced of that.

The Ogorth clan wanted to work with humans. More importantly, they wanted to be left alone to live their lives in the forest. They didn't want a war. They didn't want to take over the world.

But that was precisely what the Saganto clan wanted.

Gideon wasn't sure how they thought they could do it. They were killing many dragons, but there were so many more humans out there. If they started a war, the strength of the entire country's military force would fall on them. Even right now, there were humans scrambling to get weapons ready and training to fight against dragons. It would be a bloodbath, but they'd be ready to take on the Saganto clan.

For now, the Saganto clan was staying away from humans. They were using hunters, but they had no intention of allying themselves with any other humans. Gideon wouldn't be surprised if the clan killed all the hunters once they were done with them. They were a means to an end, nothing more. He might never have met anyone from the Saganto clan, but he knew they didn't care about humans, not even the humans helping them.

"Gideon?"

A knock on his office door made him look up. He expected it to be Jennifer, since anyone who wanted to talk to him had to go through her, but it wasn't her. It was the queen, and Gideon scrambled to get out of his chair.

She smiled and waved at him to stay where he was. Gideon watched her as she stepped in and came closer, sitting in one of the seats on the other side of his desk. It was wide enough to accommodate her in her dragon form, but thankfully, she didn't shift. It would have made the conversation quite hard.

Most of the furniture in the palace was made both for dragons and humans, and Gideon was working with what he'd been offered. He didn't mind the wide seats. They were comfortable, if a bit odd to use while working.

The queen was silent for a moment. Gideon waited, knowing she'd get to the point soon. He suspected he already knew, anyway.

"I'm sure you've heard about the clan that has been attacked," she eventually said.

"News travels fast in the palace," Gideon confirmed.

She looked worried, which was understandable, and an

emotion Gideon shared. The Saganto clan had only attacked smaller clans for now, but everyone knew who their main target was. Gideon wasn't sure what they were waiting for, and while he was glad for the respite, it also made him nervous.

"There are no survivors. I got news from another clan who lives nearby. They are terrified but still sent someone to check in on what was left." She looked straight at Gideon. "There was nothing. The clan's home burned down, and there were bodies everywhere."

Gideon swallowed. "I'm sorry." He doubted the queen had personally known anyone from that clan, except maybe their leader, but it still had to hurt. It wasn't just the knowledge that the Saganto clan was coming for them. Losing so many dragons when there were already so few of them couldn't be easy to deal with.

"I don't know what to do," the queen admitted. "I want to stop the Saganto clan, but I don't know if we can. I should be ready to sacrifice my people to ensure the Saganto clan stops hurting dragons, but how can I? I don't want anyone to be killed or hurt."

"Well, whatever you decide, the government will stand by your side."

She stared for a moment. "That's why you're here."

It was. "I've already talked to my superior. They know what's happening and are keeping an eye open, as always. We don't want the Saganto to win any more than you do." Because if they did, they would start a war with humans, and that was something no one wanted.

No, it was better to be an ally to the Ogorth clan and deal with them than to deal with the Saganto clan. Gideon still used social media and listened to human news, so he knew that many people were wary of the alliance with the dragons. They didn't understand what was happening, and they were frightened. Even though dragons had always been hidden, they couldn't keep the attacks secret. Random parts of forests and mountains were on fire, and even the humans couldn't ignore the war.

The problem was that humans viewed all dragon clans the same. Humans wanted to protect humanity, but they didn't realize that by pushing away the Ogorth clan, they would push away the only thing that still protected them. Luckily, they weren't the ones making decisions. Gideon wasn't, either. The decision makers were allies with the Ogorth clan, and that was all that mattered. Hopefully, it would be enough.

There was no way to know.

He cleared his throat. He'd been talking with his superior earlier, and he'd mentioned something Gideon had found interesting. He wasn't a soldier and wouldn't win any fight, but he couldn't deny that what his superior had told him made sense. "So far, you've allowed the Saganto clan to run wild," he told the queen. He needed to choose his words carefully because he didn't want to offend her.

"Do you think I wouldn't have stopped them if I could?" she asked.

"I don't know. But we've been hiding, which, while understandable, isn't going to work forever. We both know what the Saganto clan is doing. They're trying to get to you and your clan, and to do so they're killing other dragons. Maybe it's time to stop hiding in the palace. Maybe it's time to go on the offensive and get ready to face them."

Gideon was almost sure he'd spoken out of turn and that the queen was going to have him imprisoned or something, but instead, she seemed to be considering his words. Gideon wasn't sure he could convince her to do this, and it wasn't his role to do so.

But the Ogorth clan was his home now. He didn't want the palace to be destroyed and the clan to be killed. He didn't want to lose his new friends.

He didn't want to lose Lisha.

Lisha couldn't stay in the infirmary one second longer. Everyone who came in wanted to talk about the new attack, while he wanted to stop thinking about it. He made sure someone would be there if anyone needed help, then he made his way to the mess hall. It probably wasn't the best place to go if he wanted to avoid gossip, but he needed food. He didn't have to eat there if he didn't want to, anyway.

He needed to stop thinking about all the dragons who had died, about what the Saganto clan was doing, but it was almost impossible. No matter how hard he tried to distract himself, his thoughts always circled back to the war.

Dragons had kept themselves isolated from humans and other clans for decades. Everyone wanted peace, and that was the best way to obtain it. All that was over now. The Saganto clan *wanted* war, something everyone else had been trying to avoid. They wanted control and power and thought they could get it by using violence.

They might be right.

Lisha was glad when he reached the mess hall. It was full of people talking and eating, but Lisha ignored everyone and made a beeline for the food. His stomach growled as he grabbed a plate, and someone beside him snickered.

He turned to see Sebastian holding a plate. Sebastian grinned at him, and he found himself smiling back because how could he not? Sebastian was adorable, and Lisha's heart hurt at the thought that he might get hurt. If the Saganto clan attacked, they would kill all the humans in the palace.

"I'm hungry, too," Sebastian said as he filled his plate.

Lisha mirrored his movements. He got more vegetables than Sebastian, although he avoided the peas. He didn't like mushy peas, and he could see that these were mushy.

"Why don't you come to sit with us?" Sebastian asked when his plate was full.

He tilted his chin toward a table by the window, and Lisha wasn't surprised to see it was already full. It seemed like every human except Gideon and his people were there. Blake and his brother Sheldon were sitting with Sheldon's daughter, trying to feed her something with a spoon. Christian was there, too, the egg sitting on the table in a small blanket nest.

They were surrounded by dragons. Caven looked slightly out of place but at peace with his son in his arms. Lisha hadn't been sure about him, but he could see how much he'd changed. He only wanted what was best for the Ogorth clan, and that was what everyone needed. Cain and Dagan were also there, but Slavin, who'd been sitting next to Dagan, was getting up. He kissed Dagan on the cheek, which made his brother Orion groan and look away.

Most of those people weren't related, but they'd built a family. Watching them together made something in Lisha's chest hurt, and he realized he was jealous.

He was an only child. He'd grown up with his parents, but that was what happened to most dragons. They still lived at the palace, of course, but they rarely saw each other. Especially lately, Lisha had so much work that he hadn't visited. That wasn't the only reason he hadn't. He was never quite sure what to tell them. They were good people, but they didn't have much in common.

Lisha had always found it hard to make friends, but it seemed he wouldn't have a choice. Sebastian had grabbed his arm with his free hand and was pulling him forward. For a second, Lisha wondered if he should step away and say he needed to go back to the infirmary, but he quickly decided against it. Sebastian was trying to be nice. He was trying to be a *friend*, and that was what Lisha wanted. He'd probably make a mess out of the situation and say something stupid, but these people would ignore it. They wanted to be his friends as much as he wanted them to be, which wasn't something he was used to, but he couldn't deny it. It wasn't the first time they pulled him into a meal with them, and he felt almost like he belonged as he settled at the table next to Sebastian.

"Hey, Lisha," Slavin said as he walked behind Lisha.

He squeezed Lisha's shoulder, and Lisha turned his head to look at him. "Slavin," he said, tilting his head.

"Sorry I'm not sticking around. I'm sure you've heard the news."

"I have."

"Well, I hope you have a nice meal. Keep an eye on everyone for me, will you?"

Lisha wasn't sure why Slavin was asking him, of all people, but he nodded anyway. Once Slavin was gone, he turned his attention to the rest of the table. He nibbled at his food as he listened to the humans talk. Everyone was worried about the attack, so of course, that was the main topic of the conversation.

"I'm just saying that we're safe here," Blake said.

"I know we are, but what's going to happen if they attack the palace?" Sheldon asked. "How are we supposed to defend ourselves? We're not dragons."

His words reminded Lisha of something he'd been worried about. He was a dragon healer. He was used to healing and helping dragons, and he wasn't sure he'd know what to do if one of the humans was hurt.

He frowned as he stared at his plate. He'd been using his tablet to get books about human anatomy, but no matter how quickly he read, it wouldn't help him if one of the humans was hurt in an attack. He needed to do more, but he didn't know what. Besides, even if he knew how to take care of a

human, he'd only be one healer. He had to take care of dragons, too, and many would need him in case of an attack.

"You look a bit overwhelmed and worried," Sebastian said
as he knocked their shoulders together.

"That's because I am. I wouldn't know how to help you if
you were hurt."

Sebastian chewed on a piece of bread as he watched Lisha.
"Why don't you ask Gideon to get some doctors?"

Lisha blinked. "I'm sorry?"

"It makes sense, no? You're not a doctor. You're a healer,
and you heal dragons. I'm sure you'll be able to help me or
the other humans in a pinch, but wouldn't it be better to have
actual doctors here?"

"Where would I get doctors?"

"Ask Gideon. The government wants to help us in any way
they can. I think they're afraid of what the Saganto clan will
do if they manage to destroy the Ogorth clan. Besides, if he's
going to live here, he might need a doctor, too. You helped
him when he was poisoned, but I can't help but wonder if that
was luck."

Lisha stared at his fork. "In part. It helps that our human
form is similar to yours, but it's not the same. The poison has
the same effect on the human body as on a dragon, which is
why I was able to help Gideon." But what would have happened if he hadn't been able to?

"Talk to Gideon. Well, you need to talk to the queen, too,
unless you want the doctors to be a surprise. Considering
what's coming, I don't think anyone will say no to having
more doctors and healers at the palace."

He wasn't wrong. Lisha certainly wouldn't say no to more
help, and it would be better if these doctors could get here
before the fight reached them. If it did—*when* it did—they
would need all-hands-on-deck. They needed more healers
and doctors.

And Lisha knew who could provide them for him.

Gideon wasn't sure how the queen would take his suggestion. He knew a bit about the history of dragon clans, and he was aware that most clans kept to themselves because of a war that happened a long time ago. Isolating themselves meant they weren't fighting, which in turn meant that dragons weren't dying.

There weren't many dragons, even though there were more clans than Gideon had expected. The queen didn't want to sacrifice any dragon to the war, but the problem was that she wouldn't have a choice. The Saganto clan had taken it from her and every dragon involved, and they needed to accept that and finally do something about it.

"Do you know our history?" Queen Ita asked.

"I know about the war, if that's what you're asking. I realize it's the reason you're so hesitant about this."

She nodded. "I don't want to start a new war. The last time we were fighting, we lost many dragons. Families were destroyed. Entire clans disappeared. A new war would do the same, and I don't want to be responsible for that."

Gideon leaned forward. "But you wouldn't be responsible for it. The Saganto clan has already started a war. They've already taken out small clans and killed too many dragons to count. There is no peace. It's gone, and you had nothing to do with it. But now the war is here, and you need to decide how you're going to protect your people. I understand why hiding at the palace sounds good, and if I'm honest, I'm perfectly fine staying here, but do you really want the Saganto clan to attack? Because they will eventually. They're making their way toward the Ogorth clan, and when they get here, they won't hesitate to attack."

The queen looked at Gideon. "And you think that attacking

them first is a good idea?"

Gideon knew how careful he needed to be answering that question. "I think that we need to find out exactly what they're planning. I think we need to be ready for the attack, but at the same time, we shouldn't allow them to bring it to us. The palace is a safe place. If we have to, we can probably barricade ourselves in here for a while. The government will step in and help as much as they can, but it would be better if we weren't forced to hide. You'll lose dragons either way, your Majesty. The Saganto clan plans to kill every Ogorth clan member, and there's nothing you can do about that. People are going to die, but are they going to die fighting or hiding?"

Gideon realized that it was easy for him to say those words. He wouldn't be out there fighting dragons. He wouldn't be out there at all. But Gideon would die if the Ogorth clan fell and the palace was breached. He had no doubts about that, and he'd been aware of that fact when he'd taken the job.

He trusted the Ogorth clan to keep him safe. He wished there was more he could do to protect them. He was doing his job as best as he could, and he prayed it would be enough.

"What do you think I should do?" the queen asked.

Sometimes, it was easy to forget how young she was. She was strong and capable and guided the Ogorth clan the best way she could. She was doing a great job, but being responsible for all of this had to be terrifying, especially with the Saganto clan gunning for them.

"The Saganto clan needs to be dealt with," Gideon said slowly. "They won't stop until their leader is taken out. I doubt every single member of the Saganto clan is okay with what's happening, but they have to obey orders. If we take away the people who are giving those orders, then maybe, we can stop the war." The soldiers would no doubt be happy not to be sent out to kill dragons and possibly die. Gideon had never been to war, but he could too easily imagine how awful it was for everyone involved.

"I wish it were that easy."

"I have no doubt it's not easy at all, but the only other alternative is to hide at the palace and wait to be attacked. I don't think that's what you want."

It wasn't what Gideon wanted. This would be dangerous, and dragons would die, but from what he could see, the only way to get rid of the Saganto clan was to face them head-on.

And hope that the Ogorth clan would be the only clan still standing when the dust settled.

CHAPTER FIVE

Gideon was everywhere. Lisha had expected to see him often since he now lived at the palace, but it was getting ridiculous. It seemed like every time Lisha left the infirmary, Gideon was there. They bumped into each other in the hallway, the mess hall, and even the library.

Lisha couldn't help but wonder if it was happening on purpose.

He couldn't say he was sorry about it, because he wasn't. He wanted to see Gideon often. The human was endearing and adorable, and Lisha liked spending time with him. He liked how flustered Gideon was when they talked, how he seemed to need to fill every silence yet at the same time, how he wanted to hear what Lisha had to say. He always had a lot of questions, but he never pushed for answers. He was as content to talk about his day as he was talking about dragon anatomy.

And when they talked, his entire focus was on Lisha.

Lisha wasn't used to that. People listened to him, of course, but that was because he was a healer. They trusted him to tell them what to do so they'd heal and feel better, and he did. This situation was different because it was personal. Lisha wasn't giving Gideon instructions to heal an infection. He was telling him about a book he'd read, a movie he'd seen, or even his favorite flower.

Lisha didn't think anyone else in the world knew what his favorite flower was. He hadn't even realized he had a favorite flower until Gideon had asked, and of course, only a few days after Lisha had admitted he loved orchids, Gideon had presented him with a pink one. He'd been blushing and flustered but also looking proud of himself. Lisha had accepted the gift, and even now that he'd had the orchid for a few days, he couldn't stop thinking about it.

Gideon was courting him.

He hadn't told Lisha that was what he was doing, but it was pretty clear. He was interested in Lisha, listened to what Lisha had to say, and brought him gifts. When they spoke, he always leaned closer, as if he couldn't stop himself from doing so.

And he wasn't the only one. Lisha could admit he had a crush on the human, and it had been a while since he'd last felt that way for anyone. The problem was that he didn't know if this was the best moment to have a crush and start a relationship. He didn't think Gideon would refuse if he told him that he wanted to go on a date. If anything, he'd be all over himself to do so in a hurry. Gideon was enthusiastic, which was something that made Lisha smile.

But everything was a mess. The Ogorth clan would soon be at war, and even though neither of them would be fighting, they'd still be in danger. Gideon would stay at the palace, but Lisha would need to go out there and care for the wounded, meaning he'd risk his life. Would it be fair to either of them to start a relationship when something could happen at any moment?

Lisha didn't know. He wanted to say fuck it and give in, and why shouldn't he? If he was going to die soon, shouldn't he die happy? Spending time with Gideon would make him happy. He didn't want to think about the possibility that he'd die, but it wasn't something he could ignore.

No one at the palace could.

Lisha had noticed several new relationships between dragons. Everyone felt the need to anchor themselves and have something good before the war started. It would hurt if Lisha lost someone, but wouldn't it hurt even more to die knowing he and Gideon could have had something but fear had stopped them?

Lisha groaned and thumped the back of his head against one of the pillows in his nest.

He should be getting up and going to the infirmary, but he felt lazy today. He wanted nothing more than to stay in his nest and look at the orchid on the table by the window and think about Gideon. It wasn't a very adult thing to do, but if he didn't do it now, when could he? Once the war started, there would be no lazy days. There would only be blood and pain, and Lisha didn't want to think about that until he couldn't avoid it.

His thoughts circled back to Gideon. The man was clearly interested, yet he hadn't tried anything. He wasn't even trying to seduce Lisha. He talked to him, smiled a lot, and gave him beautiful flowers. Was Lisha reading too much into it? But Gideon wasn't gifting flowers to anyone else. He'd made a lot of friends already, but he hadn't bought any of them flowers. His behavior made Lisha feel special, and there could only be one reason for that, right?

Gideon wanted Lisha as much as Lisha wanted him.

There was only one way to find out. Lisha didn't know if he'd regret this, but he rolled out of his nest. He paused by the window to stroke a fingertip down one of the leaves of his orchid, then went to wash up. He hadn't left his nest yet today, and he was a little hungry, but he didn't go to the mess hall. It was getting late in the morning, so the breakfast food would be gone, and everyone would be getting ready for lunch. Nervousness made Lisha's stomach churn so much he wondered if he might throw up on Gideon's feet as soon as he opened the door, so it was better not to eat.

Lisha knew Gideon would be in his office. He worked a lot, and while Lisha wanted to tell him he needed breaks, he didn't dare. No one wanted to take breaks when it could mean losing the war. Today was different, though. Gideon *was* going to take a break whether he wanted it or not, because he would be having lunch with Lisha.

Or at least, Lisha hoped so.

His nerves almost got the better of him when he reached the office. He stood staring at the open door. He couldn't see into the office from here, but he could see his assistant's desk. She was talking on the phone and nodding, but eventually, she looked up and noticed Lisha. She cocked her head as if wondering what he was doing there, but when he didn't move, she returned to her phone call.

That didn't last long, since Lisha was standing there like a creep. She hung up after a few minutes, then looked at him again. "What can I help you with?"

"I was wondering if Gideon had something planned for lunch." It would be just Lisha's luck.

"No. He's not seeing anyone for lunch. Do you want me to ask him if he has time for you?"

"Please." Lisha was tempted to turn around and rush away, but it was too late.

Jennifer rose from her chair and went to knock on Gideon's door. Gideon's voice told her to come in, and she opened the door, a smile playing on her lips. She looked from Lisha to Gideon again, and Lisha had to resist the urge to push past her to see Gideon.

His crush was getting worse, dammit.

"There's someone here for lunch," Jennifer said.

"I didn't think I had plans." Gideon sounded confused, which made sense considering they hadn't had plans.

"You didn't, but I think you'll be happy with your lunch break. I'm going to go take a walk to stretch my legs. I'll see you in an hour or so."

She winked at Lisha as she walked past him. Lisha

hesitated, wondering what to do, but he didn't have to wonder for long. Gideon appeared at the still-open door, a frown on his face. It quickly vanished when he saw Lisha, and his smile was everything. He was clearly happy to see Lisha.

"Lisha. What are you doing here?"

Lisha straightened his shoulders. "I'm here to take you to lunch."

"You want to eat lunch with me?"

"I would love it. If you want to come with me, I have to do an egg wellness check first." Lisha didn't have it planned, but Gideon loved the egg. Besides, it wouldn't be a bad thing to check on it again.

Gideon's smile widened. "I would love to. We can go right away."

Lisha didn't know what he was getting himself into, but he also didn't care. He just wanted Gideon to continue smiling the way he was now.

Gideon didn't know why Lisha had thought of him for lunch, but he wasn't about to protest. He wanted to have lunch with Lisha. He wanted to check in on the egg, even though he'd seen it this morning at breakfast. Christian carried it everywhere and looked like a proud father even though the egg wasn't his.

Seeing him with the egg made Gideon slightly jealous. He wanted to be a proud father, too. When he thought about having children now, he couldn't imagine them not being born from an egg. He didn't really care if the baby was biologically his or not. Before, he'd thought about adoption, but since he hadn't had anyone special in his life, he'd never gone through with it. He was glad he hadn't because it would have complicated everything, and he probably wouldn't be here at the palace if he'd had a child.

But he wouldn't have to adopt if he married a dragon. They could have their own children, and the thought of him and Lisha having kids made Gideon's stomach flutter.

But Lisha wasn't here to have children with him. He was here to take him to lunch, so Gideon quickly went back to his office to shut down his computer and grab his phone. Lisha was still in Jennifer's office when he was done, and the way he smiled told Gideon he was doing the right thing.

He could miss a couple hours of work if it meant spending time with Lisha. They wouldn't have nearly enough time to do that once the war started, and besides, Gideon had his phone with him. If anyone needed to reach him, they could.

He really hoped no one would try calling him while he was with Lisha, though.

"What have you been up to today?" he asked Lisha.

"I've had a lazy day. There isn't a lot to do in the infirmary at the moment. It looks like everyone in the clan is healthy."

That was good, because they'd need everyone to do their part when the Saganto clan attacked. Gideon didn't want to think about that right now. It was too dark and depressing, and even though no one could ignore the reality of what was coming, it would be good not to obsess over it for a few hours. "Everyone needs lazy days sometimes," he said. "I've been known to take my fair share."

"What do you do? I didn't do much more than stay in my nest this morning."

"I like to read in bed."

Before Gideon had become an ambassador, he'd spent part of his Saturday and Sunday mornings in bed reading. He usually finished the book he'd started the night before, then finally rose and got on with his day. Now that he was here at the palace, he sometimes had to work, but he always tried to find an hour or two in which he could have some peace. Everything would be easier once the Saganto clan had been dealt with, and he couldn't wait to have a new routine.

He hoped that this lunch date and Lisha's questions meant Lisha was interested in him. Gideon was pretty sure he was, but he was having difficulty reading the healer. Lisha seemed interested, but he was also keeping some distance between them, and Gideon didn't know why. Maybe it was because Lisha didn't want to start anything with a war looming, but as far as Gideon was concerned, if not now, when?

They deserved to be happy and have something to come back to. They deserved to continue living their lives as if the war wouldn't happen. They deserved to have someone they could think of while the war raged around them and someone they could come home to once it was over.

And Gideon wanted that someone to be Lisha.

He didn't want to come on too strong, so he didn't say those words out loud. Lisha was skittish, but he was getting better, and the last thing Gideon wanted was to freak him out. So instead of declaring his undying love for Lisha, he followed him to Christian's room.

"I haven't told Christian I was coming," Lisha said as he rubbed the back of his neck.

He knocked on the door, and something screeched loudly inside. Gideon took a step back when he heard hurried footsteps coming toward the door, then something slamming against it. The door opened, and a harried-looking Christian looked out at them.

He frowned. "Lisha? Did I forget a visit?"

"You didn't. I just wanted to check on the egg if that's okay."

Something peeked from behind Christian's back. It took Gideon a moment to realize it was Christian's nephew, and when he did, he grinned at the baby. He was in his dragon form, which was as adorable as his human form.

"I don't mind, but I have the babies."

Lisha blinked. "All of them?"

"Yeah. I guess Sheldon and Morven wanted some time together. When Hogan and Cain learned about it, they left Lorne here, too, and Sky was already here."

"We can come back later."

Christian looked slightly panicked at the thought. "No, *please*. Come in."

Gideon almost laughed. Christian loved the babies, but it was understandable that having most of them together couldn't be easy, especially if he was alone. Ruy would have helped, but he was probably at work, meaning Christian was alone.

Or rather, he had been.

The babies were on Gideon as soon as he walked in through the door. He recognized them now, so he knew who was who. Sky, who'd been on his uncle's back, quickly hopped off to land on Gideon's shoulder. The other two clustered around him, both of them in their dragon form.

They were adorable.

Gideon dropped to the floor. He was here to see the egg, but he could play for a bit while Lisha examined it. That way, he'd keep the babies occupied, and Lisha could have the space he needed.

Lorne rolled onto his back in front of Gideon, making him laugh. He scratched his stomach, making him wiggle. Nothing should be as adorable as a baby dragon. They could bring anyone to their knees with just one look.

Gideon lost himself in the babies. He didn't know how much time had passed, but when he eventually looked up, it was to see Christian and Lisha sitting next to each other on the couch. Christian was cradling the egg, and they were both looking at Gideon.

Gideon's cheeks flushed. "Sorry about that."

"You have nothing to be sorry about," Christian told him.

"You gave me a much-needed moment of respite. And while seeing you being so good with them makes me want a baby of my own, considering my morning, it's going to have to wait."

"They're just incredible, you know?"

"I know," Christian agreed.

Gideon hadn't come to play with the babies, but he was glad he had. Having them treat him like an honorary uncle made him feel he was part of their family, giving him even more reason to fight for them. These babies were the future of the Ogorth clan. Some of them had both a human and a dragon father, and hopefully, they were the first of a long line of hybrids that would lead the Ogorth clan and keep peace with humans.

But that could only happen if they defeated the Saganto clan. Gideon didn't know what he'd have to do to make sure that happened, but whatever it was, he would. He wouldn't let anyone hurt these babies and their fathers.

Or Lisha.

It wasn't just Christian who had a sudden urge to have a baby after watching Gideon with them—Lisha felt like if he'd been fertile at the moment, he might have thrown himself at Gideon and begged him to have a child with him. He was so good with the babies, and the sight of him handling them so carefully made Lisha want to give him anything he wished for. He didn't care if it was babies, a palace of his own, or something else. Lisha just wanted him to be happy.

He hadn't expected this to happen when he'd decided to ask Gideon out for lunch, but they'd still have enough time to eat, and Gideon looked more relaxed after playing. Lisha had taken advantage of the fact that the babies were distracted to check in on the egg, and it was perfectly healthy. It wasn't ready to hatch yet, but it looked like it hadn't been hurt through everything that had happened since it had been laid.

The baby would never know their parents, but they would be healthy and loved. Lisha couldn't give the child their parents back, but he could make sure they had a long and happy life. He wouldn't be the only one to do so. Everyone was ready to defend this baby and the others with their lives.

"He's good with them," Christian said. "Really makes me want a child."

"I thought Ruy wanted to wait."

"He does, and so do I. I don't want him to get pregnant in this kind of situation. Besides, he's not fertile at the moment, and he told me it wouldn't happen for a while."

He wasn't wrong. Who would want to bring a child into this world when it might be destroyed? Yet as Lisha looked at Gideon, he couldn't help but wonder what their children would look like. They'd take their color from Lisha, but it would be lighter. The children wouldn't be bronze like him, but they'd be beautiful anyway. Maybe they'd have Gideon's warm brown eyes or his nose. They might need glasses, which would be odd on a dragon, but Lisha would give them anything they needed.

But he and Gideon might never have kids or get together, and they couldn't tell what the future would be like.

"What about you?" Christian asked with his gaze still on Gideon. "Have you ever thought about having children?"

It was as if he could read Lisha's mind. "This would be the worst moment to have children or start a relationship," Lisha murmured.

"I agree with the children part, but not the relationship one. What better moment than to fall in love?"

"The war is about to start," Lisha pointed out as if Christian didn't know.

Christian rolled his eyes. "I'm very much aware of that. But it's not like you can stop your feelings from growing, and once you're in love, losing someone will hurt whether you're with them or not. At least if you're in a relationship, he can be happy before it happens. Besides, who said you'd be hurt? You and Gideon won't be fighting."

Neither would Ruy, but some of their friends would be out there. Morven, Slavin, Hogan, Octavia, and all the others would be facing the Saganto clan, and the thought made Lisha want to throw up. Maybe Christian wasn't wrong. Lisha wasn't in a relationship with any of them, but he still felt sick at the thought of something happening to them. If something did happen, he would be in pain because he would have lost a friend.

If something happened to Gideon, he'd be destroyed because even though they weren't together, he was starting to fall in love with him.

Lisha needed to stop hesitating so much. If he wanted something to happen between him and Gideon, then he needed to take a chance. He didn't think Gideon would reject him, and while they might lose each other, the feelings were already there. They'd be hurt even if they decided to ignore what was growing between them.

Lisha couldn't imagine a life without Gideon. He wanted the light touches, the smiles, the care Gideon put in every moment they spent together, and to stop second-guessing himself. He wanted a future with Gideon, and while it was as terrifying as the thought of losing him, Lisha needed to take a leap of faith. He needed to believe that everything would be all right and that once all of this was over, he and Gideon would settle down and be happy. He didn't know what their relationship would be like or if they truly would share their futures, but that wasn't what mattered at the moment.

What mattered were the feelings Lisha had for Gideon—and of course, the feelings Gideon had for Lisha.

Chapter Six

Gideon was used to living with the dragons by now. He was used to having many people around him, to the many voices and bodies filling the palace, and to the amount of gossip flying around. That was why he could tell that something was happening when everyone started buzzing with anticipation. He'd been minding his own business and thinking about Lisha and the lunch they'd shared, but he couldn't ignore it anymore. He couldn't even fake he was reading the news on his phone while having breakfast. It was too distracting.

The room felt like it would explode with excitement. He looked up, trying to find the reason for what was happening.

Luckily for him, Slavin happened to be grabbing a plate when Gideon glanced up. As soon as he'd filled it, Gideon waved at him. He didn't know where the others were this morning, but with the children, they probably needed more time to get everything ready before breakfast.

Slavin didn't have kids. He and his partner were both there, and by the time they sat with Gideon at his table, Gideon was sure something was going on.

"Please tell me you don't have bad news," he begged.

Slavin grinned. "Nope. Killian is visiting."

Gideon knew the name, but it took him a second to place it. "The Eiloren clan king?"

"Yup."

"Isn't that unusual?"

As far as Gideon knew, dragon clans tended to stay away

from each other. Things like that were bound to change since they were at war, but it was still odd to think that another leader was visiting, even though Killian had been here before.

"Killian and the queen are friends," Slavin said as he shrugged.

Dagan leaned forward. "Some say they're more than friends."

Slavin wrinkled his nose. "I don't think so. Besides, how would that work? They lead two different clans."

Gideon couldn't say he wasn't interested in that kind of gossip, but he couldn't focus on it. "When is he arriving?"

"Not sure exactly when, but it's today."

"It is," a voice confirmed from behind Gideon.

Gideon turned to smile at Morven. "Good morning."

Morven nodded. "Good morning. I was looking for you."

Gideon hoped it wasn't because he was in trouble. Morven's tone made him feel like he was a schoolboy, but he hadn't done anything that would get him in trouble. "Oh?"

"The queen wants you there when she meets Killian. We don't stand on ceremony with him and his clan since we're so close, so there won't be any parties or anything like that. He's coming to talk to the queen and start planning our next steps, and both she and I agree that you should be involved."

That was probably a good idea since Gideon represented humans. It was why he was here, and he was excited at the thought of being in that meeting.

He'd never thought about diplomacy becoming his life, but that was what had happened. Being an ambassador didn't just mean being a link between humans and dragons. It meant living here, feeling like a part of the clan, and wanting to be a clan member. Even if he got fired, he wasn't going anywhere unless the queen ordered him to get the fuck out. His future was with the clan, and no one would be able to convince him otherwise.

But the longer he managed to keep his job, the better it would be for everyone involved.

"I'll be there. When do you need me?"

"In an hour."

Gideon quickly finished his breakfast after Morven left. He said goodbye to Slavin and Dagan and rushed to his room, already texting Lisha to let him know what was happening. He was proud of being included, and he wanted Lisha to know.

The entire palace is talking about the visit, Lisha texted back.

I'll be sitting in on that meeting.

Good. They'll need your help.

Gideon wasn't sure there was anything he could do for the queen or Killian, but that wouldn't stop him from trying.

He changed clothes, even though he was already wearing dress pants and a shirt. He wanted to make a good impression on the king. He was pretty sure the queen wouldn't care even if he went to her meeting in sweatpants and an old t-shirt, but he didn't know Killian as well, and he didn't want to risk it. He made sure his tie wasn't crooked and that his jacket fit well, and by the time he was done, it was time for him to head out.

His footsteps traced the path to the queen's office. Gideon spent a lot of time there, maybe as much as he spent in his own office. He was here to help the queen, and he liked talking with her. She was intelligent and had common sense. He hoped all of that would be enough for her to defeat the Saganto clan.

A guard stopped him before he reached the door of the queen's office. They waved Gideon toward the throne room doors, and Gideon nodded in thanks. When the guard opened the door, he stepped in, holding his breath, but there was no one there yet. The queen was on her throne, with Caven standing next to it. They were talking, but they both looked up when they heard Gideon, and the queen smiled.

"I'm glad Morven was able to find you," she said.

"Thank you for inviting me to this meeting," Gideon said, bowing slightly. "I'm excited to meet Killian."

"And he's excited to meet you. The Eiloren clan doesn't have humans, and he's always delighted when he gets to visit with them."

"They're not animals in a zoo," Caven muttered.

Gideon was pretty sure Caven had never been to a zoo, but he wasn't wrong. Gideon and the other humans weren't animals to gawk at, but thankfully, that wasn't how Gideon felt when dragons wanted to spend time with him. He was just as curious about them as they were about him.

"Stop being so grumpy," the queen chided her cousin. "No one will do or say anything to Sebastian. He's a taken man, and the two of you have a child."

The grumpy expression vanished from Caven's face, replaced by a smile.

That made Gideon yearn, although he wasn't sure for what. Maybe for someone to come home to at the end of a long day? Maybe for *Lisha* to come home to at the end of a long day?

The doors behind Gideon opened again. He turned to see the same guard stepping in, but before the guard could announce the visitors, a tall dragon pushed past them. He was smiling widely, his focus on the queen, but he stopped when he noticed Gideon.

"Another human?" he asked, sounding delighted.

Gideon lightly bowed. "Your Majesty, my name is Gideon. I'm the human ambassador to the Ogorth clan."

Killian grinned. "I knew I'd meet you this time around. I'm Killian, and I order you to call me that."

Gideon found himself smiling. He didn't know Killian yet, but he could tell they'd get along just fine. "Of course, Killian."

The king nodded, clearly satisfied. "And this is my assistant, Tito," Killian continued as he gestured behind himself. "The two anchors dragging behind me are Marlin and Birch."

They behaved like bodyguards and were clearly unhappy at being called anchors. It was an interesting dynamic, and as Gideon settled in for his first meeting with the Eiloren clan king, he couldn't help but have hope.

The Ogorth clan wasn't doing this on their own. They had Gideon, the government, and many other clans who didn't want the Saganto clan to win. Gideon had to believe it would be enough. He had to believe that together, they could defeat the Saganto clan.

He wouldn't have it any other way.

"Your boyfriend is meeting with the queen and king," Sheldon teased.

Lisha didn't have to ask what Sheldon was talking about. Like everyone in the clan, he'd heard that the Eiloren king was visiting and that he'd been enthusiastic about meeting Gideon. Once, Lisha wouldn't have thought twice about such an occasion, but knowing that the king wanted to meet Gideon made him feel jealous, something he didn't like.

He shouldn't be jealous. Gideon wasn't his, no matter what Sheldon said.

But Lisha *wanted* him to be his. They hadn't talked yet, and he was still hesitant about the whole thing, but the thought of possibly dying without ever getting to kiss Gideon made Lisha panic. He'd decided he would talk to Gideon, but he wasn't going to do that today.

He leaned back in the chair and cradled Lorne against his chest. "Not my boyfriend."

Lorne snuffled and settled harder against Lisha's chest. Baby dragons were adorable, but even more so when they were asleep. The babies had been playing all morning, and they were exhausted now that it was lunchtime. Sheldon and the others had been feeding them when Lisha had arrived in the mess hall, but it hadn't lasted long. As soon as he'd sat down with them, Lorne had climbed into his lap and promptly fallen asleep. Lisha had stared at him for a moment because he didn't understand what was happening, but then he'd rolled with it.

Apparently, he was a great pillow.

Sheldon leaned over the table. His daughter was in her human form, held against his chest by a sling. "He's not your boyfriend? Could have fooled me. The looks the two of you give each other are almost enough to set the palace on fire."

Cain snickered. "None of that, please. I like my home to be intact."

Lisha rolled his eyes. "I won't deny Gideon and I have been spending a lot of time together, but he's not my boyfriend. We're just friends."

"For now," Sheldon said with a grin.

Lisha considered his options. He could deny there was anything between him and Gideon, but everyone around the table would know he was lying. Apparently, it was clear in the way they looked at each other.

His other option was to admit he had a crush on Gideon and wanted him. No one here would care. If anything, they'd probably be happy for him. They would push him into doing something about it, and he wasn't sure he was ready for that, but he was running out of time. The Saganto clan wasn't going to wait until Lisha got his shit together to attack. They weren't at the Ogorth clan's door yet, but it wouldn't take long.

He sighed. "Fine. I like him."

"And I'm pretty sure he likes you," Sheldon added.

"I don't know. We haven't talked about it, and I don't

know if we should."

"You're scared," Cain said gently.

"I know there isn't a right moment to start a relationship and that the war shouldn't stop me because I deserve to be happy, but I don't want to be a distraction. Gideon needs to focus on his job."

Which was what he was doing today. From what Lisha had heard, he'd walked into the throne room this morning and hadn't reappeared yet. Lunch had been taken in there, so it would be some time before Lisha saw him.

He desperately wanted to go knock on that door, but he wouldn't. His place wasn't in the throne room with the king, the queen, and the ambassador. His place was here, surrounded by his friends and their children. He and Gideon could see each other later.

Hopefully.

"I guarantee that if you mention liking him, he's going to jump you," Christian said as he waved his fork at Lisha. "He's been watching you with heart eyes since you saved him from the poison."

"You think he likes me only because I saved his life?"

Christian looked at Lisha like he was an idiot. "No. I think he likes you because you're handsome, smart, driven, and caring, and also a little bit because you saved his life. You made him feel like he was worth saving. Besides, you didn't just save him. Even after he was better, you stayed by his side and kept him company. Anyone else could have done it. I remember volunteering to do it, but you waved me away and said it wasn't necessary."

That was because Lisha had found out he liked spending time with Gideon. It was then that his crush had started, and it wasn't getting any better. If anything, it was getting worse.

Luckily for him, it seemed Gideon liked him just as much. Neither of them was doing anything about it for now, but that would change. Lisha didn't know what he'd do if it didn't.

Maybe scream?

He looked down at the baby in his arms. "Thank you," he whispered.

He wasn't used to people giving him compliments. His parents had when he was younger, but these days, people expected him to heal them since he was a healer and the queen's personal healer at that.

More than that, Christian seemed to see him beyond his healer role. It wasn't something Lisha had expected, and it made him realize that the people around the table considered him more than a friend. They'd been including him in their meals and gatherings because they wanted to spend time with him, and he could never say no. It would be like telling his parents he wouldn't be coming for dinner.

They weren't friends. They were family.

Christian grinned. "You're welcome. Now, are you going to do something about Gideon?"

And they were back to talking about Lisha's love life. "Eventually."

Christian waved the fork again. "You'd better hurry because you won't have any time left if you wait too long." He hesitated, then looked at the others around the table. "No one here wants you to rush into something you might not want, but we all know what's coming. When *that* starts, we're all going to need something to cling to, something to remind us of what we're fighting for, and there's nothing better than love to do that."

Lisha looked at the baby in his arms again. Christian was right, but he didn't need to be reminded of what he was fighting for. Everyone at the palace loved their families, their freedom, and their lives as they knew them. Even if Lisha didn't have Gideon, he'd want to survive for his parents and his friends, and he'd want to fight for the babies. He had plenty of things to return to once the war ended.

But somehow, adding Gideon to that list felt like a good thing to do.

Gideon was exhausted and incredibly excited at the same time. He still had a hard time believing everything that had happened this morning, and he was going to need a few hours tonight to wrap his mind around it.

The queen had treated him like she always did. He didn't fully understand why, but she seemed to view him as a friend and someone she could trust. He was glad she did and had promised himself he wouldn't do anything to betray her trust, but he hadn't expected the king to behave the same way.

When Gideon spoke, Killian listened. It wasn't out of politeness. The king was *actually* listening to what Gideon was saying. He considered every word without hesitation, and that made Gideon feel important and like he was doing something to change the outcome of the war. It also made him feel like the king respected him and his role as ambassador, which he hadn't realized he needed.

He'd never planned to become an ambassador and wouldn't have been if the queen hadn't specifically requested him for the role. When she had, Gideon's superiors had scrambled to put everything into place and teach him what being an ambassador meant. The problem was that there had never been an ambassador to a dragon clan, and everyone had known it wouldn't be the same as being an ambassador to another country. There were similarities, but the dragons needed to be handled differently.

Gideon thought he was doing a good job, and from a few things his superiors had said early in the conference call they were on, he wasn't the only one. It made him feel satisfied because he hadn't known if he'd be any good at this job.

But he was. He'd been doing his best, and it felt good. It would feel even better once the Saganto clan had been dealt with, though, which was what they'd been focusing on.

And now he needed to focus on what was going on in the room—he and his team were in the middle of a conference call. The king and queen had called other clan leaders, and together, they were going over what was happening and what they could expect from the Saganto clan. Everyone had agreed that something needed to change before the Saganto clan destroyed all of them. The Ogorth clan was massive and had many members, but most of the other clans were much smaller. They knew what awaited them if the Saganto clan turned their attention to them.

"I don't want the Saganto clan to destroy my home and my people," one of the clan leaders said. "They've killed too many dragons already. We can't allow them to continue."

"I agree," Killian said.

It was still weird to think of a king by his given name, but the few times Gideon had slipped and called him *your Majesty*, he'd glared at him until he corrected himself. Gideon had gone over the information he had about every leader on the call, which wasn't much, but he knew that Killian had only become king recently. It was the worst time for anyone to become a king, but he was dealing with everything as best as he could and, in Gideon's opinion, splendidly.

"Your clan is big, and you have a special relationship with the Ogorth clan. Nothing is going to happen to *you*," another dragon said.

Gideon glanced at his notes. He'd written down everyone who was participating in the call, and he knew that this person was Leopold. Apparently, he hadn't been happy when Ita decided to ally with the humans, but after the Saganto clan had led the hunters in the attack of the meeting of clans, he'd changed his mind. He was snarky and a bit bitchy, but he was

71

on the right side.

"The relationship between our clans doesn't change anything," the queen said. "As long as you're one of our allies, if something happens to you, we'll step in to help."

"And even if you're not in an alliance with us, as long as you're not working with the Saganto clan, we'll help," Killian added, glaring at the phone on the queen's desk. "Being so close to the Ogorth clan might put my clan in even more danger, but I won't back down, and neither should anyone on this call. The Saganto clan will only be stopped by fighting them, and no one here can do so on their own."

They needed to stop bitching at each other. It wouldn't do anyone any good, although, in this situation, Gideon wasn't sure he'd be able to stop them. The king and the queen might listen to him, but the other leaders? Even though they had an alliance with them, he was nothing to them.

He cleared his throat. He might not be able to stop them, but he could redirect the conversation. "The government has been looking into the hunters. Last I heard, they've already arrested a dozen of them. It's not all of them by any means, but it's still a dozen fewer people in the war."

"That's good," Killian said with a nod. "We haven't fought against humans in a long time, much longer ago than the war between dragons. As long as you take care of the hunters, we'll take care of the Saganto clan."

That was the plan. The dragons would focus on the Saganto clan, and hopefully, between the Ogorth clan, the Eiloren clan, and their allies, they'd have enough dragons to defeat them. As far as Gideon and the government, they'd focus on trying to arrest as many hunters as possible before they could reach the palace. However, Gideon had no doubt that some would, which was where the military came in.

He swallowed. "As I said, we'll do what we can to stop them before they get here, but we might not be able to stop all of them. As long as everyone agrees, my superiors want to send several teams as support."

Gideon and the queen had already talked about it, and while she was hesitant, she'd agreed. There were a few conditions, but nothing Gideon couldn't deal with. He didn't need the approval of the other leaders since the teams would be staying with the Ogorth clan, but it would be good if everyone was on board with this.

"More humans?" Leopold said, spitting out the last word as if it disgusted him.

"We'll take all the help we can get," the queen said coldly. "We'll need everyone in this fight, and that includes humans. They don't want to make enemies out of us and certainly don't want the Saganto clan to win this war. You won't have to worry about them, anyway. As Gideon said, he and his people will focus on fighting the hunters. They'll be on foot in the forest, while we'll be in the air."

They would need to meet several more times to settle the details, but they had a plan. It was more than they'd had when the meeting started, and Gideon felt good about this and the war's outcome.

They would win. They had to.

CHAPTER SEVEN

M ore humans were coming. Once, Lisha would have been worried about it. He still was, a little bit, but they were coming because they were going to defend the clan, and now that he knew the humans who lived with the clan better, he wasn't as wary. He realized they might not accept dragons the way Sheldon and the others did, and they might even be disgusted or scared, but as long as they helped with the Saganto clan, he didn't care.

The fight was inching closer every day, and the palace was frantic with activity. It was even busier today because the teams that would help deal with the hunters were arriving. Gideon had promised Lisha they were sending several doctors, too, and Lisha hoped they wouldn't be afraid of him and that they'd listen to what he had to say. Even though these doctors would focus on the humans, they'd still be working out of Lisha's infirmary, and Lisha wanted them to get along. They didn't need to be friends, but they did need to be able to work together.

Everything was settling into place. The humans were coming, and the clans were working together. They still didn't know when the Saganto clan would attack, but at the moment, they seemed focused on smaller clans, which gave the Ogorth clan some respite. That wouldn't last forever, and Lisha was terrified, but they were doing their best with what they had, and it was all they could do.

The arrival of these humans would be a welcome distraction, even though a lot of dragons Lisha had talked to were worried. They'd gotten used to having Sheldon, Sebastian, and the other humans around, but these were new people. No one knew how they'd react, even though Gideon had tried to reassure Lisha. Worrying about what the Saganto clan was doing didn't help, and Lisha felt like he was ready to vibrate out of his skin.

That was one of the reasons he was happy when Gideon appeared in the infirmary. The other reason was that he liked spending time with Gideon. He'd spend all of his days with him if he could, but for now, they were sneaking moments when they could. It wasn't always easy, but they made it work, and it gave Lisha a warm happiness that helped him through his days. They hadn't talked about what they were doing, but Lisha was done resisting his crush.

He hoped Gideon was, too.

"Am I bothering you?" Gideon asked as he looked around.

Most of the beds were empty. A few patients were present, but they were doing well, and Lisha had already checked in with them today. "No. Did you need anything?" he asked with a smile.

"I was wondering if you were ready to take a break."

While the patients Lisha was keeping an eye on were okay, someone needed to stay with them. He opened his mouth to say just that, but someone beat him to it.

"You can go," Atha said. "I'll stay in the infirmary over lunch and make sure everyone eats. You should take a few hours."

"I don't need a few hours to eat lunch," Lisha said as he narrowed his eyes at her.

She ignored him. "Then go take a walk somewhere. Enjoy the gardens while you can."

A pang of sadness hit Lisha. If the Saganto clan attacked the palace, the first areas that would suffer were the small gardens on the side of the mountain. Lisha spent a lot of time there, and his heart bled at the thought of seeing them destroyed. Maybe Atha wasn't wrong, and he needed to spend some time there before everything changed.

Gideon smiled and nodded. "I'll make sure he eats something and puts his feet up for a moment. Some fresh air will do him good."

Lisha was looking forward to spending time away from the chaos and noise of the palace, so he didn't resist. He was leaving his patients in good hands, so he wouldn't have to worry about them or anything else.

He only had to worry about Gideon.

They stepped out of the infirmary, but Gideon stopped. "I told your friend I'd take you to one of the gardens, but I don't know which one you prefer. I also don't think I've seen all of them, so I'll let you lead the way."

"I'll show you my favorite."

Gideon beamed. "Please."

They'd be able to spend some alone and uninterrupted time there. Hardly anyone ever went to this specific garden because it was reserved for the queen and whoever she allowed in. Sometimes the babies played there, but it would be deserted during lunchtime. Lisha was allowed to spend time there because he was the queen's personal healer, and they were somewhat close, and he was excited to show Gideon around.

"How have you been doing?" Gideon asked as they walked.

"Fine, considering everything. It's a lot to take in and deal with."

"Everyone's on edge."

"Yes. People snap at each other even though there's no reason for them to. They're also more distracted, and it leads to dangerous accidents."

Gideon frowned. "The infirmary was almost empty."

"That's because, thankfully, none of those accidents have been bad. One of the cooks cut herself with a knife, and another got burned. Someone else fell down the stairs. They're small domestic accidents, but there have been a lot of them, and I know it's because everyone's so nervous."

Gideon sighed. "I wish there was more I could do."

"Everyone is doing everything we can. It's all we can ask for and do, and it has to be enough."

But Lisha couldn't deny that sometimes it didn't feel like it was. He was a healer, so he focused on healing, but was it enough? Would it be enough once the Saganto clan attacked? He wouldn't find out until it happened, and he disliked not being able to plan.

He already knew the clan would lose dragons. Some would be wounded, and some would die. Others would never recover from what would happen to them, no matter how hard Lisha worked. Lisha wished he could magically make everyone better, but that wasn't how healing worked. He'd already seen enough horrible wounds on the survivors who were still trickling in.

The Ogorth clan and their allies had to be careful when they went in after learning another clan had been destroyed. The Saganto clan might still be there, waiting to ambush them. So far, they'd brought back several survivors, dividing them between the various clans. Lisha had never before seen the kind of wounds the survivors sported, but he was quickly learning how to deal with them. He'd studied them in theory, but as long as there had been peace, there hadn't been that kind of injuries — the bite and claw marks, the flesh torn apart, the missing limbs.

Peace was over. He needed to learn to deal with that, and he was, even though it gave him nightmares.

"The Ogorth clan will make it out of this," Gideon tried to reassure Lisha. "You're not alone. You have allies, and together, we'll defeat the Saganto clan."

Lisha nodded because he had to believe all of it. He had to believe that by the end of the war, the Ogorth clan would still be standing and capable of rebuilding.

But he was afraid.

Gideon was glad when Lisha stopped in front of a door. They'd had an important conversation as they walked, but he'd wanted to see Lisha and take him away from the infirmary so they could both distract themselves. Everyone was thinking about the war twenty-four seven. It wasn't too much to ask to have an hour to look at flowers and talk to Lisha, was it?

Lisha nodded at the guard standing by the door and pushed it open. Gideon hadn't expected the guard, so as soon as they were outside and the door was closed behind him, he turned to Lisha. "Why a guard? Is the queen afraid the Saganto clan might try to come into the palace through one of these doors?"

As far as Gideon knew, she wasn't. The door did lead into the castle from the outside, but the gardens were tucked into the side of the mountain. They were open to the sky, but not so much that people wouldn't notice dragons landing there. Besides, no dragon would come close enough to be able to do so without someone noticing and sending guards to stop them.

"The guard is there because this is the queen's personal garden," Lisha explained. "Only she and the people she authorizes are allowed in here. Your new friends and their babies are, but they'll be in the mess hall at the moment. We should have the garden to ourselves."

Gideon was impressed, even though maybe he shouldn't be. Lisha was the queen's personal healer and the head of all the healers in the palace. It was a prestigious role, so it made sense that he was allowed in this peaceful corner of paradise. The queen trusted him with her health and her son's, so why not with her garden?

He looked around. He was surprised to see trees, but maybe he shouldn't be. The dragons were ingenious, and it wasn't the first time he noticed they'd worked something out to make the palace feel like a small city. Most of the dragons flew out at least once a day, but for those who couldn't or didn't want to, the gardens were a space where they could be outside without actually leaving the palace.

There was even a fountain, but that wasn't what caught Gideon's attention. No, that was all Lisha.

He led the way between the trees and plants, pointing at things as he talked. Gideon wasn't sure what he was saying, mostly because he kept losing himself in his voice and the way he looked.

He wanted this dragon almost desperately. He didn't want to freak Lisha out, but waiting until the war was over felt like the worst possible thing to do. Gideon didn't know if he or Lisha would die or if something would happen to them. He didn't want to think about that possibility, but he couldn't ignore it, either. If something were to happen to them, or if God forbid, the Ogorth clan lost the war, Gideon didn't want to die with regrets. He wanted Lisha, and he was pretty sure Lisha wanted him. Why wait?

A relationship might be a distraction, but it might also be what gave them the strength to fight harder. It was all Gideon could think about as he watched Lisha, and he wondered if they'd have another opportunity to be together alone like this. With every day that passed, the Saganto clan moved closer. Eventually, they would be so close that the fight would begin, and then, there would be no time left. Even if the Ogorth clan won, it would take some time for them to pick up the pieces and fix everything the Saganto clan had ruined. There might not be a place for love and time spent alone.

Which meant Gideon had to make the most out of this moment. He stopped in the middle of the path.

Clearly absorbed in what he was looking at, Lisha didn't respond right away. Finally he turned to look at Gideon. When Gideon didn't join him, Lisha moved back, a frown marring his beautiful face. "Is there something wrong?" he asked.

Gideon loved him. There was no ignoring it or lying about it. It was how he felt, and he was terrified that he would never have the opportunity to tell Lisha. The problem was that he didn't know *how* to tell him, but maybe he didn't have to use words. Maybe leaning forward and kissing Lisha was enough.

So that was what Gideon did. He didn't touch Lisha except his lips, which wasn't easy considering he had to rise on his tiptoes because of Lisha's height. He brushed his lips against Lisha's mouth, the light contact enough to send a spark of desire running through him. He quickly took a step back.

Lisha didn't let him go far. One of his hands shot out and curled around the back of Gideon's neck. He didn't pull Gideon closer, but they stared at each other for a moment. Lisha's eyes were wide.

Gideon told himself it was because he was surprised and not because he was thinking about the many ways he wanted to beat him up. The fact that Lisha was still staring without saying anything made him jittery, so he opened his mouth to make a joke and lighten the tension.

That was when Lisha kissed him.

The touch wasn't as light this time. They clearly both knew what they wanted and what the other wanted, and Lisha pressed his body against Gideon's. He was taller and had to lean down, which couldn't be comfortable, but he didn't complain. He pressed his lips against Gideon's once, then a second time, and Gideon opened his mouth to him.

He wanted Lisha so much. He wanted him so badly that sometimes, not having him made him feel empty. It couldn't be healthy, but nothing in their situation was right now. They were dealing with the knowledge that one or both of them might die soon. They were panicky with need, want, and fear, and they were doing things that maybe they wouldn't have done otherwise.

Gideon would have wanted Lisha anyway, but he would have done this differently if the situation had been different. He'd have asked him out on a date, maybe organized something in this very garden.

But the kiss was perfect anyway. It didn't matter that they didn't know what the future held.

They could do this. Together, the Ogorth clan and their allies would defeat the Saganto clan. They would lose people and might even lose the palace, but the victory would be theirs.

It had to be.

Lisha was only half surprised by the kiss. He'd wanted to kiss Gideon for a while now, and he'd been pretty sure the same went for Gideon. He just hadn't known where and when it would happen, but it couldn't have been more perfect. He loved this garden, and he was half in love with Gideon. It didn't matter that the world was on fire. They were in each other's arms, and only that mattered.

Lisha pressed closer to Gideon, wanting more but not knowing *how* much more. He'd never been very interested in sex, and he'd always thought that maybe it didn't matter to him as much as it mattered to other people. He wouldn't call himself asexual, because when he did have sex, he enjoyed it, but he'd never felt the drive to sleep with people just because he found them attractive. He'd never felt like he'd die if he didn't have sex.

But he did feel like he might die if he didn't continue kissing Gideon.

Maybe he wasn't asexual. Maybe he was demisexual and needed to be in love before wanting someone. He did want Gideon, but he wouldn't care if they never had sex, either.

He didn't know what he was, and it didn't matter. How he felt about sex was the least important thing about him. What mattered was who he was, what he did, and who he loved.

"You don't know how long I've wanted to do this," Gideon murmured.

"Probably as long as I've wanted to."

Gideon laughed. "Are you okay?"

Lisha snuggled against Gideon, pressing his face against Gideon's neck. It probably looked ridiculous since Lisha was much bigger, but that didn't matter. No one else was here, and even if they hadn't been alone, Lisha would never feel ashamed of his feelings for Gideon. Gideon was a bright soul who was doing everything he could to help dragons even though he was human. It would have been easy for him to dismiss the clan, to refuse to work with them, and to treat them like little more than animals, but he hadn't. From the first day, he'd treated them like equals, something very few humans had ever done. It was one of the things that had attracted Lisha to him and one of the things that had made Lisha love him.

As far as he was concerned, Gideon was perfect. Now that they'd kissed once, he wanted to continue doing so forever. It was probably too much to admit right after their first kiss, though, so instead, Lisha breathed in and out until his heart stopped racing.

Then Gideon kissed him again, and Lisha's heart jumped.

Was this going to happen every time they kissed? Or would it eventually become routine? Lisha felt that wasn't possible, but what did he know? He'd never felt this way for anyone but Gideon. He didn't *want* to feel this way for anyone else ever again. Gideon was his everything, the center of his crumbling world. Lisha needed to cling to him and ignore what was happening outside the palace's walls at least for an hour. He needed Gideon to be his rock in the storm, the one place where he would always come back because it was his home.

Lisha kept those words to himself, too. He didn't want to freak out Gideon, even though he suspected Gideon felt the same. Those words were better left unsaid, at least for now.

But that didn't mean they couldn't be together, and they continued kissing for what felt like hours. When Gideon eventually stepped away, Lisha almost chased him. It made Gideon chuckle, and while Lisha glared at him, there was no heat in it.

"Come on. We should take a walk," Gideon says, holding out his hand.

Lisha stared at him for a moment, trying to understand what he wanted. When he didn't move, Gideon huffed and grabbed Lisha's hand to pull him down the path.

They were holding hands.

It was all they were doing, yet it felt incredibly intimate. The gesture was casual, but it also had a deep meaning that made Lisha want to purr and curl around Gideon, both in his human and dragon forms.

They walked in silence for a while, and Lisha was content. He could forget the war raging outside the palace's walls for the next hour. He could ignore the fact that the Saganto clan would attack and try to destroy them. He could ignore the fear that something would happen to Gideon and that he'd lose him.

Lisha didn't know what would happen, but he was

convinced he'd make it through. He wouldn't face the fight alone. He had Gideon to come home to, as well as their friends. More than friends, they were like a family, and Lisha had never felt so loved.

And *that* was what mattered. Love was what pushed the Ogorth clan to fight the Saganto clan. Love was what would eventually lead them to victory.

Lisha had plenty of love to give and the most perfect man to give it to.

CHAPTER EIGHT

Lisha was hiding. He couldn't stand having lunch in the mess hall when everyone was talking about the latest attack. The Saganto clan had once again targeted a smaller clan, and there had been no survivors. Everyone was gone, and there was nothing Lisha or anyone else could do to help them. So many lives were cut short just because the Saganto clan wanted power.

It wasn't fair.

Lisha knew that eventually he'd have to come out of the infirmary. His friends would no doubt wonder what had happened to him. He and Gideon had made a point of eating lunch together as often as they could since their first kiss in the garden, so he would, too. It wasn't that Lisha didn't want to see them. It was more that he was overwhelmed and felt powerless, and he didn't know how to deal with that.

He was a healer. His job was to help people in need, but in this case, there was nothing he could do. Even if he'd been allowed to go to the destroyed clan, there were no survivors for him to heal.

He didn't think he'd ever hated anyone, but he hated the Saganto clan. At this point, he didn't even care that some of the members were probably good people who were forced to do what they were doing because otherwise they would die. Wouldn't it be better to die than to kill innocent dragons? To take babies away from their parents and raise them in pain and hate? He didn't know how the Saganto clan dragons could live with themselves, and he didn't think he would ever understand it.

The sound of footsteps running toward the infirmary got him to his feet. He was used to the urgency. Being a healer, people ran to get him every time an accident happened, and with so many dragons living together, it happened often. Lisha had already grabbed his bag and was ready to go by the time the guard burst into the infirmary.

The guard looked around, their focus stopping on Lisha, who was moving toward them.

"What is it?"

"We're bringing in a male."

Lisha nodded and put down his bag. It probably wasn't as bad as he'd feared if the dragon could be moved. "What happened?"

"We don't know. He's in bad shape, though."

"Who is he?"

The guard shook their head. "I don't know."

It didn't make sense. Even though there were many Ogorth clan members, most of them knew each other, at the very least by sight. The guards especially kept an eye on everyone, so why wouldn't this one know who the wounded dragon was?

The dragon couldn't have come from the latest destroyed clan. There'd been no survivors, so it wasn't possible. It didn't sound like he was an Ogorth clan member, either.

Who did that leave?

There were more footsteps, and Lisha focused on getting everything ready. Luckily, the infirmary was never empty, and the nurses were a great help. They got one of the beds ready, and Lisha rushed toward the hurt dragon as soon as he was carried into the infirmary.

While Lisha wasn't a guard, he knew most of the people who lived with the clan. He saw many of them because of illnesses and injuries, and even when he didn't, he knew them through their families. Even if a parent had never needed his help, their child would have.

But he didn't know this dragon. He was a very light green, almost too light to be called a color. Lisha sucked in a breath when he realized who this dragon was.

The egg's second parent. He had to be.

The dragon was awake. His eyes were open and he stared at the ceiling, but the way he was reacting worried Lisha. Sure enough, when he pressed a hand against the dragon's forehead, he felt he was burning up. His eyes were glazed over, and he appeared confused.

Everyone got into motion. Lisha ordered several exams, and as the nurses helped him, he leaned closer to the dragon's head. "My name is Lisha. I'm the Ogorth clan head healer. Can you tell me your name?"

The dragon opened his mouth, then frowned. "Alix."

"How did you end up in my infirmary this morning?"

"I don't know." Alix licked his lips. "They chased us."

Lisha wanted to ask questions, but he needed to focus on Alix's body. It was worse than he'd expected, and he was worried the dragon wouldn't make it.

Suddenly, Alix grabbed Lisha's wrist. He was squeezing so hard that it hurt, but instead of pulling back, Lisha leaned closer.

"What is it?"

"We lived with the Saganto clan. We ran away after we realized Merial was pregnant. She's from the Eiloren clan." Alix looked back at the ceiling. "Where is she?"

Lisha's heart squeezed. He wanted to tell this dragon that everything would be all right and that he could see his family once he felt better, but it would be a lie. He'd lost his mate. She'd died, and while the egg was fine, Lisha could see why Alix had a fever. Countless claw and bite wounds covered his body, and several had gotten infected. Lisha would attempt to save him, but he was afraid that Alix was too far gone—his body was ravaged by the infection.

Once again, Lisha was powerless. He couldn't save this dragon. He couldn't give him his family back. He could only help him not feel pain as he passed away.

Lisha didn't care that Alix was a Saganto clan member. The Saganto clan had hunted and killed his mate and, ultimately, him, as well.

"She's fine, and so is your egg," Lisha lied.

"Yeah? Are they back with the Eiloren clan?"

"Is that where you were headed?"

Alix nodded. "She has a cousin there. Tito. He's the one who convinced us to leave the Saganto clan, even though we were terrified. He said we would always have a place with the Eiloren clan, even though I was born in the Saganto clan."

Lisha remembered that name. "The king's assistant?"

Alix grinned, which looked odd considering, well, everything. "Yeah. He's a bit stuck up, but he's a good guy. He'll keep them safe." He frowned. "I need to tell you something."

"You can tell me anything you want."

Lisha glanced up, and he and one of the nurses looked at each other for a moment. She shook her head, and while he wanted to rage at the unfairness of all of this, he couldn't. His focus needed to be on Alix and taking the pain from him. Lisha and the nurses were giving him medicines that would fight the infection, but they wouldn't have enough time to work. He was dying.

"They're going to attack," Alix croaked. "We heard them talk about it when we left the clan. They're going to attack the Ogorth clan."

Lisha's stomach churned. He felt guilty about trying to get information considering the situation, but it sounded like it was one of the reasons Alix had stuck close to the palace.

The guards had still been looking for the egg's second parent. They'd finally found him, which meant he hadn't been too far from the palace. Maybe he'd been looking for his mate and their child, or maybe he'd been looking for the Ogorth clan. Either way, he was here now.

"Do you know when they'll attack?" he asked.

Alix's voice grew softer as he explained. Lisha never looked away from him, and when it was clear there was nothing more he could do, he took his hand and stayed by his side. They were pumping Alix full of painkillers, so at least he wouldn't die in pain. That didn't help Lisha feel any better, though.

The guard who'd come in first stood next to them the entire time, listening to the details Alix gave them. It wasn't much, yet at the same time, it was everything. They didn't know how many dragons would attack, but they knew when. They knew that the Saganto clan was planning to ambush the Ogorth clan, and while it would be soon, they had time to get ready.

Eventually, Alix's voice faded, and he closed his eyes. The guard still hovered there, but Lisha shook his head at him. "Go and tell the queen what happened."

"He might wake up and give us more details."

"He'll never wake up."

The guard's expression was grim, but he nodded. He glanced at the dying dragon before turning around and rushing out of the infirmary.

The other guards had vanished earlier, and the nurses had taken a step back when Lisha had ordered them to. Having them hover around Alix wouldn't help.

But Lisha wasn't going anywhere. He'd hold Alix's hand until he stopped breathing. Only then would he allow himself to break down.

A knock on the door made Gideon look up. He hoped it was Lisha disturbing him in his office, but when the door opened after he called out, he saw it was Slavin.

His expression must have told Slavin what he'd been thinking, because the big dragon smiled. That didn't last long, and Slavin's expression turned grim.

"What happened?" Gideon asked as he got to his feet.

It was clear *something* had happened, although it was a daily occurrence these days. There was always one more clan that fell, more dragons who died. Gideon loathed feeling powerless, but he was only one human. He was doing every-thing he could to keep the Ogorth clan safe, but unfortunately, everything he could do wasn't enough.

"The guards found the egg's second parent," Slavin ex-plained.

There could only have been one outcome to the situation if Slavin looked so somber. "They died?"

Slavin nodded curtly. Gideon had expected that, but it still hurt.

The egg had been with them for too long for its parents to be all right. They'd been in the forest, possibly wounded, run-ning for their lives. Gideon had hoped, but when weeks had passed and nothing happened, he'd known.

And now, he knew he was right.

"He died here in the palace, in the infirmary," Slavin said. "Lisha was with him until the end. He and a guard managed to get some information from the dragon, so we know he came from the Saganto clan. We confirmed he was the egg's father."

Gideon swallowed. "Lisha was with him until the end, wasn't he?"

"You know him. He wouldn't have wanted the dragon to die alone, and he would have wanted to make sure he couldn't get any more information before he passed."

Gideon's heart hurt for Lisha. He was a healer, and it couldn't be easy for him to watch people he desperately tried to save die. Gideon had been thinking that *he* was powerless, but he couldn't imagine feeling the way Lisha had when he'd realized there was nothing he could do to save this dragon, no matter how long and hard he tried.

"I need to go to him," Gideon declared.

"It's why I came to you. I knew you wouldn't want him to be alone."

"Is he still in the infirmary?"

"From what I've been told, he's behaving as if nothing happened and seemingly decided to go through with the rest of his day."

Gideon clicked his tongue. Of course that was what Lisha was doing. He'd want to wait until he was home tonight to allow himself to break down. He wouldn't want anyone to see that.

There was no doubt in Gideon's mind that he would break down. Lisha had a soft heart and never dealt well with death, but then who did? Death was hard and unjust, especially in this situation. The Saganto clan was killing so many dragons, and while Gideon wasn't sure of what had happened here, he was ready to bet they were involved. Who else would these parents have been running from? Who else would have hunted them this close to the Ogorth clan palace and killed them on their doorstep?

It was one more reason to make the Saganto clan pay, and while Gideon wouldn't be the one to hurt them physically, he had every intention of being an integral part of the group of allies who would take them down.

He and Slavin left his office together, but Slavin headed down the other side of the hallway. Gideon rushed to the infirmary, steeling himself against what he'd find. Lisha would behave as if nothing had happened, but he'd be bleeding inside.

He knew he was right when he peeked in through the open

infirmary door. Lisha was talking to a patient, acting like this was just another normal day. He was even smiling slightly, but Gideon could see the heartbreak in his eyes. The patient looked like they didn't know something was off, but Gideon did, and he had to resist the urge to grab Lisha and drag him out.

He was an ambassador, a diplomat. He could do this without offending anyone and causing Lisha to yell at him for interfering.

"Are you ready for our lunch date?" he asked as he walked in.

They tried to have lunch together every day, but sometimes it wasn't possible. Gideon had had a conference call at lunchtime, so he hadn't eaten yet. He wasn't hungry, though. He just needed to get Lisha out of the infirmary.

Lisha blinked at him. "What are you doing here?"

"Well, my conference call is over, and I don't think you ate. I thought maybe we could grab something and go to the garden."

Lisha's jaw set, and he looked at his patient. "I have work to do."

The dragon in the infirmary bed patted Lisha's hand. "I'll be here when you come back. I wouldn't say no to having lunch with such a handsome man, if I were you."

Gideon wasn't sure how he should feel about the dragon complementing him, so he limited himself to smiling and nodding. He could see that Lisha was going to argue, so he didn't give him the chance. He grabbed his hand and pulled him toward the door, ignoring his indignant yelp.

"What are you doing?" Lisha asked as Gideon dragged him through the hallways. "I told you I can't do this. I have work."

"And I told you that you needed to get lunch."

They wouldn't get to the garden fast enough, so Gideon

took them to his office instead. Jennifer was nowhere to be seen, which was good, but Gideon still locked his office door behind them.

They were alone, and as he turned to look at Lisha, he could see the dragon was about to break. Gideon was afraid to touch him in case he was the one who caused the breakdown, but he still reached for him.

Lisha threw himself into Gideon's arms. Gideon took a step back as the weight hit him, but he stood strong as Lisha pressed his face against his neck and started sobbing.

Gideon's heart broke along with Lisha's. He wanted to do more for him, to heal the pain of losing a patient, but he couldn't. He could only make soothing sounds as he stroked Lisha's back and promised everything would be all right.

He was pretty sure Lisha didn't allow himself to be this vulnerable with anyone else, but at the moment, knowing that didn't bring him the satisfaction it should have. He didn't want Lisha to be vulnerable. He didn't want him to feel so bad that he burst out crying as soon as they were alone.

But there would always be patients who didn't make it. In this case, it had been especially horrible because of the circumstances, but Lisha had to be used to losing patients. Whether or not he was, it didn't matter. For as long as he cried, Gideon would be there with him, holding him and doing whatever he could to make him feel better. It might not be enough, but it was all Gideon had to offer.

And he hoped it would be enough.

Lisha had lost patients before, but it had never been like this. He wasn't sure why this had hit him so badly, and he didn't know if there was an answer to that. Maybe it was the war, or maybe it was because he felt close to the egg, but whatever the reason, Lisha couldn't stop feeling like he should have

He couldn't have. Even if he'd gone out into the forest to try to find the egg's parents, nothing he could have done would have changed the outcome for that family. He'd done the only thing he could have done and had helped Alix pass away peacefully. He'd lied to him and had promised that his family was fine.

Eventually, the tears dried up, but Lisha stayed where he was, pressed against Gideon's chest. His neck hurt because he needed to lean down so far, but he didn't care. Even though he was bigger and could turn into a dragon, he felt safe and cherished in Gideon's arms and never wanted to leave them.

But he had to. He was an adult and a healer, and his people needed him.

With regret, he stepped away from Gideon. He should have known Gideon wouldn't let him go easily, though. He could be stubborn when it came to Lisha, and while Lisha didn't fully understand why, he liked it. He caught Lisha's hand so Lisha couldn't run away like he was tempted to, and Lisha couldn't avoid looking at him.

"Better?" Gideon asked.

Lisha opened his mouth to say yes, but instead, what came out of his mouth was a croaked, "No."

Gideon didn't look surprised. "Why don't I take you to your room? You can freshen up and take some time to breathe."

There was nothing Lisha wanted more. He had responsibilities and things to do, but right now, nothing was more important than licking his wounds in private and taking some time to breathe. He felt he might break if he didn't, and that wouldn't help anyone, least of all the people he was supposed to help.

"I'd like that." What Lisha would like even more would be to spend more time with Gideon. Maybe if they were together for a few hours, Lisha would be able to forget the pain Alix's death had caused. He wanted to lose himself in Gideon, and while it might not be fair to ask that of him, Lisha wasn't sure he could stop himself from doing so.

Gideon either didn't realize how much turmoil Lisha was in or had decided to ignore it for now, because he took Lisha's hand and pulled him out of his office. Lisha felt exposed now that they weren't alone anymore, but thankfully, no one looked at him as if they thought something was wrong. They passed several dragons, but everyone was either in a rush or busy talking to other people.

Gideon and Lisha reached Lisha's rooms without having to talk to anyone. Gideon paused in front of the door, and Lisha brushed past him to open it. This time, he was the one who dragged Gideon along. He didn't want Gideon to leave, now or ever. It was too soon to say that out loud, but maybe Lisha could make it so that Gideon would know anyway.

As soon as the door was closed behind them, Lisha turned and grabbed Gideon. Gideon made a startled sound, but Lisha swallowed it with a kiss that made Gideon moan next. The reaction he had to Lisha was exhilarating, and Lisha didn't know how he'd lived without this man until now.

"Make me forget," he whispered against Gideon's lips. "Please."

"Are you sure?"

Lisha nodded. He *was* sure. There was no one or nothing he wanted more than Gideon, and while the circumstances might not be perfect, it didn't matter. He knew what he wanted, and that was Gideon. That wouldn't change once this was over, or next week, or next month.

Thankfully, Gideon didn't ask a second time. He trusted Lisha to know what he wanted, and while Lisha didn't have any details in mind, as long as he got Gideon naked and in his nest, he'd find a way to make it work.

They kissed again. Gideon made delightful noises that Lisha didn't know how to deal with but wanted more of. He moved them as they kissed because stopping felt impossible. Lisha yearned for Gideon, and he finally had him.

They stumbled into the nest room. Gideon tripped on his own feet, but Lisha was strong enough to hold him up. He did so by wrapping his arms around Gideon and hauling him into his arms, which had Gideon making a delicious sound that went straight to Lisha's groin. He felt his pouch starting to open, and he knew that soon, Gideon would be confronted by Lisha's anatomy. The thought that he wasn't used to it gave Lisha pause, but Gideon continued kissing him.

Lisha took a step back. Gideon looked delicious, and Lisha couldn't look away. Gideon's cheeks were flushed, and his lips slick. His glasses had slid down his nose, and he pushed them back up as he stared at Lisha with wide eyes.

"I'm not human," Lisha said.

Gideon blinked as if he didn't understand what Lisha was saying. "I'm aware."

"That means my . . . organs are different from yours."

Gideon's gaze slid down Lisha's body and stopped at his groin. His cheeks flushed deeper, and Lisha's pouch released a burst of slickness. He was ready to take Gideon inside his body, but he wasn't sure that was what Gideon wanted. There was no way to know how Gideon would react to his body, either.

Gideon licked his lips as he continued staring. Lisha couldn't stop his body's reaction, and when his cock slid out of the pouch, he just stood and allowed Gideon to look. That way, if Gideon wasn't comfortable going further, they could stop before making him freak out.

But Gideon didn't look freaked out. He was still staring, maybe because he'd never seen anything like this, maybe because he found Lisha attractive and wanted him. Lisha wrapped his fingers around his cock, deciding to give Gideon a little show. He was pretty sure that even if Gideon had hang-ups about this, they could work them out. It wouldn't be enough to push them apart, but Lisha *really* wanted Gideon to like what was in front of him.

"I can see that," Gideon whispered.

Lisha ran his finger up and down his shaft, spreading the slickness. The inside of his pouch pulsed with need and felt empty, but Lisha was scared. What if he reached for Gideon and Gideon pushed him away? Lisha needed to seduce him. He had to make himself look appealing.

He shouldn't have worried.

He didn't know what to expect when Gideon finally moved, and he watched as the man he loved nearly strangled himself in the haste to take off his tie. Gideon swore and threw it across the room as if it had offended him, then started pulling on his shirt. His fingers trembled as he unbuttoned it, and Lisha realized that Gideon wanted this as much as he did.

That was all he needed to know.

He let go of his cock and wrapped his fingers around one of Gideon's wrists. Gideon froze, possibly expecting Lisha to stop him, but that wasn't what Lisha was planning on doing. Instead, he quickly slid Gideon's shirt open before Gideon could tear off the buttons. He could get more shirts, but that didn't mean he had to tear this one to pieces.

Gideon wasn't as careful as Lisha. He pulled off his belt, then fought with his trousers for a second. Lisha had never been so happy to be a dragon shifter who didn't wear clothes. He didn't have anything to pull off before he could have Gideon.

Gideon made a frustrated noise when his pants fell to his ankles and pulled off his shirt. He tried to step forward but couldn't, and Lisha had to keep him upright as he fought with his shoes and pants. He was still wearing his underwear, and

Lisha slid a hand into it to cup one of his ass cheeks.

Gideon froze, but only for a second. Then he kicked his pants away and grabbed Lisha's cock without hesitating, showing Lisha he wasn't afraid or disgusted.

Lisha groaned as Gideon's hand moved on him. His fingers were soft but not too gentle, squeezing Lisha's flesh as he explored it. He didn't seem intimidated by the slickness that kept on coming from Lisha's slit. Instead, he gently dipped his fingers into the pouch, making Lisha shudder in pleasure. He slid his fingers back up Lisha's cock, then back down again.

His touch disappeared. Lisha blinked and looked down to see that Gideon was reaching behind himself. Lisha had watched human porn after he'd realized he and Gideon would eventually do this, so he knew Gideon needed to be prepared. He seemed to understand what Lisha needed without Lisha having to tell him, and it was sexier than anything Lisha had ever seen. He should be doing that, but he couldn't look away.

He had to when Gideon kissed him. Their tongues tangled, and even though Lisha didn't like coffee, he enjoyed the taste of it on Gideon's tongue. He enjoyed many things if Gideon was involved.

Gideon pushed against Lisha as if he was trying to get closer. There was only one way to make that happen since they were already plastered together, so Lisha grinned and slid the hand he didn't yet have on Gideon's ass around and down his body. He pushed the underwear out of the way — asking himself why Gideon hadn't just taken it off — and cupped Gideon's other ass cheek. He could feel Gideon's hand move between his cheeks, and he could too easily imagine what it looked like, even with the underwear still covering him.

Gideon squeaked when Lisha hauled him into his arms

and twisted to the side. Lisha stumbled toward the nest, almost falling but clutching Gideon to him so he wouldn't drop him. He only did so when he felt the softness of his nest under his feet, and even then, he first lowered to his knees.

Gideon had pulled his fingers out of his body to cling to Lisha, but he reached between his legs now. Lisha leaned back to look at what he was doing, and his brain froze.

Gideon was the most beautiful man Lisha had ever seen, and Lisha couldn't believe he was his.

He couldn't look away. His pouch pulsed, and his cock jerked. He wanted Gideon in any way he could get him.

He rubbed his fingers inside his pouch, biting on his lower lip so he wouldn't cry out, and slicked them up. When he reached for Gideon, with his flushed cheeks and crooked glasses, Gideon spread his legs, offering himself up to Lisha.

Lisha pushed a finger into Gideon while taking off his glasses with his other hand. They kissed again, and something settled deep in Lisha's chest. His heart still hurt, but being with Gideon was like spreading a balm over the wounds. It would take time, but they would heal, and Lisha would be even stronger than before because he wouldn't be alone anymore.

He knew he never would.

When Gideon wrapped his arms around Lisha's neck and pulled him on top of him, Lisha knew he was ready. He was still slow and careful as he finally pushed inside of Gideon's body because he never wanted to hurt him.

He could tell that Gideon was in some pain because he tensed, so he stopped moving, but Gideon would have none of that. He pulled again, and Lisha slid inside him as if he were coming home. Gideon welcomed him, wrapping himself around him, and Lisha knew that neither of them would ever let go. This was it for both of them, and if they both survived the war, they'd build a life together.

"I love you so much," Gideon whispered against Lisha's lips.

"I love you," Lisha said on a gasp.

In the position they were in, with him fucking into Gideon, it didn't take long for Gideon's cock to slide inside of him. Lisha's body tightened around him, and Gideon cried out. Their rhythm faltered, and it took them a moment to find a new one, but once they did, it was heaven. They brought each other to the edge of pleasure, then over it as their bodies clenched together. It was a maddening sensation—Lisha was filling Gideon while Gideon filled him, pushing into him and clenching around him at the same time. Lisha couldn't have resisted, no matter how hard he might have tried.

So he didn't. He let go, and a sob tore from his throat as he filled Gideon. Gideon cradled him in his arms as if he could tell Lisha needed it, and even though Lisha had to be squashing him, he didn't push him away. Instead, he rolled them to their sides and continued holding Lisha as he broke down again.

He wasn't frightened or ashamed. Gideon had seen him through his tears earlier, and he would now, too. Lisha trusted him, and he allowed himself to cry the rest of his feelings out because Gideon would keep him safe.

Gideon wanted to give Lisha everything he needed and wished for. Hopefully, that was what he'd done, but he couldn't help but wonder if it had been the right thing to do. Lisha had needed him, but what would happen now that he'd had him?

Gideon couldn't ask. Right now, Lisha was too vulnerable and hurt. His heart was soft, and he'd need to shield it again before he could face the world. That didn't include Gideon, and he was more than happy to stay in the nest with Lisha, holding him and giving him time to wrap his mind around what had happened and to settle down.

The world would still be there in an hour or even tomorrow. Considering how fast news traveled around the palace, Gideon wouldn't be surprised if everyone knew about what happened to the egg's father by now. Lisha would no doubt have to answer a few questions, maybe even from the queen, but for now, he and Gideon were in their own bubble. The world was outside, and they were in. No one was bothering them, and they could stay wrapped up in each other for as long as they wanted.

"Thank you," Lisha whispered against Gideon's chest.

They were still tangled together, although they'd each slipped out of the other's body. What they'd done had been unexpected but beautiful, and it had felt so much better than Gideon could have dreamed of. He couldn't believe they'd get to do this again, but damn if he wanted to.

Gideon stroked his fingertips down Lisha's spine. He'd always thought Lisha was beautiful, but he was even more convinced of it now. He'd never seen anything as gorgeous as Lisha making love, and he couldn't wait to see it again. Even if they didn't, he wouldn't care. As long as Lisha was happy, Gideon was willing to sacrifice a lot, including regular sex.

It wasn't like he'd had regular sex for most of his life. He'd always been a bit of a loner, and while he had friends, he was bad at keeping up with them. It meant he often drifted away from them and had to start from the beginning.

But that wouldn't happen with Lisha. Gideon would be there for him until Lisha didn't need him anymore, and even beyond that. Hopefully, he'd be there when Lisha breathed his last breath.

But that was too far down the future and not something Gideon needed to focus on now.

"You have nothing to thank me for," he said as he kissed Lisha's soft hair.

"You didn't have to do any of this." Lisha looked up. "I didn't force you, did I?"

Gideon snorted. "I wanted to do this since the first time I saw you. I was fine taking things slow and getting to know each other, and I'm fine doing this on impulse, too. I would have told you if I hadn't wanted it, and you would have backed down."

"You have so much faith and trust in me."

"Of course I do. You took what you needed, which is what I wanted to give you. It's what people who love each other do, isn't it?"

"You love me?"

"You know I do. Come on, Lisha. I've been following you like a lovesick puppy since I arrived at the palace. Everyone can see how much I care about you. I was just waiting for you to catch up, and you finally did." And Gideon couldn't be happier, although he couldn't help but wish the circumstances were different.

Lisha wasn't feeling well now, but that would change soon. He'd want to go back to work, and they'd have to deal with this new normal the Saganto clan had created. Then there would be the fight and everything else.

But for now, they were still in their bubble, and Gideon had every intention of enjoying it for as long as he could. Even once it burst, he wouldn't be going anywhere. As far as he was concerned, he and Lisha were in this forever.

CHAPTER NINE

L isha had expected tears when Christian walked into the infirmary carrying the egg. If he was honest, he wasn't feeling great about this, either, and he hadn't been the one who'd taken care of the egg until it was time to hand it over. It had been easy to come to care for it, even though it was little more than an inanimate object at the moment. It held so much promise, though, and while Lisha was glad to see the egg and its baby going to a family who would love them, it still hurt.

He'd seen the baby in the shell. He'd watched them move. He'd worried about them and their parents.

He'd done everything he could for that family, but it still didn't feel like enough. He wanted to give the egg its parents back, but they were gone. Hopefully, the baby wouldn't feel their absence too keenly, and their new family would tell them about the people who'd brought them into the world.

There was no one better to do so than the Eiloren clan. Lisha had been there when Tito had been told about his cousin. He'd remembered her, and that they'd played together as children, and he'd been worried about her. She'd moved to the Saganto clan to be with the dragon she loved, running away from the Eiloren clan because it wasn't something that was done, and the king had refused to let her go. Back then, each of those clans had been as bad as the other. No one had gone to get her back, and she wouldn't have followed, anyway. She'd chosen to be with Alix, and hopefully, she'd been happy during the time she had with him.

Tito had been bewildered when he'd been told that his

cousin had laid an egg and even more so when he'd realized what it would mean for him. He'd tried finding another way, but eventually, he'd caved in and had promised he would take care of the egg.

It was all Lisha and Christian wanted. The egg would be with family, and the baby would be raised in a home their mother should never have left. She wouldn't be dead if she'd stayed, but she also wouldn't have been happy with Alix, so maybe everything was as it should be.

Christian settled the egg on one of the beds, careful as always. He stared at it for a moment, and Lisha gave him the time he needed. He understood how Christian felt. They both knew this was the best outcome for the egg, but it didn't mean they wouldn't miss the little thing.

Christian stayed quiet as Lisha reached for the egg. He checked it one last time, happy to see that the baby was growing. Tito would have time to settle down and find a way to make things work before the egg hatched, and hopefully, when it did, he and his family would be ready to welcome the baby.

"Everything looks good," Lisha murmured.

Someone cleared their throat nearby, and he and Christian both turned to see that Tito had arrived while they were focused on the egg. He stood staring at the egg in Lisha's hands as if it was about to explode.

Lisha couldn't imagine this was an easy thing to deal with. Tito had lost his cousin, and at the same time, he was suddenly becoming a father. He might not be the egg's biological parent, but that wouldn't matter. He'd be the one to raise the egg, and it wasn't an easy responsibility to take on. Thankfully, he had, but it meant his entire life was about to change in a way he hadn't expected or planned for.

"I know you told me about the baby, but I almost hoped you were kidding," Tito said.

Lisha gently set the egg back onto the bed. "Unfortunately, I wasn't. This baby lost both of their parents and only has you left."

Tito snorted. "Way to make all of this sound easier. You don't have to guilt me into accepting the egg. I'm taking it home."

"Good. I realize what we're asking of you isn't easy. I'm sorry for your loss."

Tito was still staring at the egg. "You sure they wanted me to take care of it? Because Delia's parents would be happy to raise their grandchild."

"It's what the egg's father told me before he passed away. I don't know if the two of you ever met, but he seemed to know and trust you."

Lisha was slightly worried because Tito looked so panicky, but he told himself to give the dragon time to get used to the idea he was now a father. Besides, even if Tito couldn't deal with this in the end, it wasn't like he'd abandon the egg in the middle of the forest. The baby would be with the Eiloren clan, and that was where they would grow up. Their parents wanted them to grow up with Tito, but even if they didn't, they'd be with their family and surrounded by people who cared about them.

"As if I needed more responsibilities," Tito muttered, but at the same time, he moved forward. "I never met Alix, but I knew of him. I was worried about Delia, of course, but I also wanted her to be happy, and that would only have happened with Alix. That's why I didn't try to stop her when she left. I wish I had now, but then, I think that she would have hated it. She didn't deserve to die or any of this, but she made her choices, for better or for worse."

Lisha could only imagine how overwhelming all of this was, so he gave Tito space. Tito's hand trembled as he reached for the egg. He sucked in a breath when his fingertips touched the surface, but his touch became stronger and more secure after he stroked it for a moment. It was as if now that he'd touched it, he knew he could do this for sure.

He looked at Lisha. "Everything is all right? Is the baby healthy?"

"I checked, and the baby's growing perfectly. They still have a few weeks, so you'll have time to get back to the Eiloren clan and settle things."

"You make it sound easy."

"I know it won't be. It's a heavy responsibility, especially considering what's happening around us." Tito was the Eiloren king's assistant, which meant he'd be close to one of the central actors of the war. He wouldn't be in the fight, but if things went wrong, he'd be one of the first to be killed. Thankfully, he'd be back with the Eiloren clan, but with everything so unsure, Lisha felt he couldn't breathe right. He was so fucking worried for everyone that it kept him awake at night, even after Gideon distracted him.

Tito turned his attention to Christian. "I was told you found the egg and took care of it."

"I did. I was running for my life and found it in the forest. I knew I couldn't leave it there, so I brought it home and kept an eye on it."

"Thank you. If it weren't for you, this child would have been alone in the forest and would have probably died. You saved their life."

Christian looked like he was about to start crying. "It was a pleasure. Well, it wasn't, because I wish the baby's parents hadn't died, but you know what I mean. I did what anyone would have done."

"I'm not sure that's true, so thank you again." Tito cradled the egg against his chest. "I should go. I have more work to do before I can leave and return to the Eiloren clan. None of this was supposed to happen, and we're scrambling to find a way to work things out."

Christian stepped forward and reached for the egg but didn't touch it. Instead, he looked at Tito, asking for permission. Tito nodded, and Christian gave the egg one last cuddle before stepping back.

"The bodies are ready whenever you are," Lisha whispered.

Tito's expression set. "I'll take them back to the Eiloren clan. Alix might not have been born there, but his child will be, and this baby deserves to know their parents are close by and that they were loved."

Lisha had prepared the bodies so that they could be flown back, and he was glad all of this was over now. It felt like closing a chapter of an awful story, and while it wasn't over by any means, at least Alix and Delia could rest in peace.

Christian and Lisha watched Tito leave. Once he was gone, Lisha turned to Christian, not surprised to see he was crying.

"You and Ruy will have children," he said gently. "I know this was hard, but it was the only thing we could do. The egg belongs with the Eiloren clan."

Christian dried his tears. "I know. I'm just going to miss them, which doesn't make sense since it was only an egg the entire time. I got attached to it, though."

"Of course you did. You found the egg when you were in a vulnerable position, and having it helped you get through it. It makes sense that you'd want to keep it, but you did the right thing."

"Do you want kids?"

"Eventually."

Lisha surprised himself with that answer. He'd never really thought about having children. He was always busy with his job, and it felt like adding even more stress to his life.

But having children with Gideon? That would be like a dream come true and worth the added stress.

Gideon was nervous. He wasn't sure why, except that he'd seldom been in such a position of power and control in his career. He still thought he shouldn't be the coordinator of this thing, and he was glad that he'd have his team leaders to help him. He was pretty sure most of them thought he was useless, but he didn't care. Let them think that. He'd show them that he knew what he was doing.

Mostly.

"Sir," one of them said, nodding at him.

Gideon looked around the office. He wasn't meeting all the soldiers sent to help the clan. That would have been over-whelming, so he was glad. The team leaders gave him enough to deal with, and there were only a handful of them.

But they crowded his office, and even though they were technically supposed to obey his orders, he knew they didn't consider him a superior. After all, he wasn't part of the military and had no clue what he was doing.

"I want to thank all of you for being here," he said. "I know you probably didn't think you'd have to live with a dragon clan, but they need you and are grateful for your presence."

"We're doing our jobs," another man said.

Gideon tried to remember their names, then peeked at the tags on their chest. He felt he should them, but he wouldn't have that much contact with them. Once this meeting was over and during the fight, they'd be talking to Morven and his people. They'd coordinate everything from the security room, while Gideon wouldn't have a say in the battle. He was an ambassador, and his job was to be a liaison between humans and dragons, nothing else.

He was glad. He wouldn't have known how to win a war.

"Let's go over the data we have on the hunters," Gideon said.

The tension in the room was heavy. Even though every leader appeared stoic and like they couldn't care less they were here, Gideon imagined it wasn't easy for them to have to live with an entire clan of dragons. The dragons were wary, as were the leaders and their soldiers. So far, everyone seemed to get along well enough, but it would be too easy for something to happen and fights to break out. Gideon hoped that wouldn't happen, but only the future would tell. Everyone had orders and was on the same side, but that didn't mean no one would be an idiot.

"As I already mentioned, we found out about the Saganto clan's plans to attack," he explained. "They'll take to the air since it's what they're good at, but they'll be sending the hunters on foot. The hunters will attack the palace from its base by coming in through the forest. That's where you and your teams will be hiding and will take out the hunters before they can reach us."

Gideon leaned back. He'd given the start to this meeting, and now, he could relax and listen as people who actually knew what they were doing planned and thought of everything.

The queen had decided to strike first, which Gideon hadn't expected after she'd been so hesitant. It was a relief. Now that they knew what the Saganto clan was planning, they knew where the clan would be. They also knew when the clan was planning to attack, which meant they could attack first, and hopefully, the element of surprise would play to their advantage.

Gideon wouldn't be part of that. He'd stay at the palace, hiding and praying Lisha and their friends would all come back. He almost wished he could go with them, but he wasn't an idiot. He'd end up dead and distract people who would have better things to do than to keep him safe. No, it was better for everyone if he stayed here and watched the fight from afar. He wouldn't be the only one. The other humans had already told him they expected him to be with them and the babies. No one wanted to think about the possibility of the Saganto clan reaching the palace, but the babies needed to be protected if they did. Not all the guards would be fighting, but they might not be enough, and that was where Gideon, the other humans, and Cain would step in.

Gideon prayed they wouldn't have to.

It was almost time. Everyone was frantically running around the castle, getting everything ready, but it wouldn't be for long. Just a few days, and they'd attack the Saganto clan. Hopefully, they'd destroy it, and it would never be a problem again.

Gideon supposed he had high hopes, but how could he not? A happy future at the palace with his friends and Lisha was just within reach.

He just had to get rid of the Saganto clan first.

Lisha wished he could have left the infirmary with Christian. It would have been better than doing what he was doing now — getting everything ready for the fight.

It was the first time Lisha and the other healers would find themselves in this position. They'd consulted with the human doctors who'd arrived with the soldiers, who were used to going to war. They'd made a list of things the healers needed to keep in their bags and organized everything so that anyone wounded could be brought back to the castle as soon as possible and taken care of. Lisha would be on the battlefield, though, helping the wounded, stabilizing them for transport, and hopefully saving them. That was why he was stuffing his bag with everything he would need for open wounds and much worse things.

Things he really didn't want to think about until he

absolutely had to.

The thought of what he'd see on the battlefield was terrifying. It wasn't only that the clan would hurt people Lisha knew and was friends with. The marks he'd found on the bodies of the egg's parents and on the survivors, who'd reached the Ogorth clan, had given him insight into what the Saganto clan did, and it would be worse during the battle. There would be amputations, blood, and death.

He swallowed and decided now wasn't the right time to think about that. He couldn't avoid it forever but could do so for as long as possible. He had no idea how to deal with any of this, and he prayed he wouldn't break down on the battlefield when people needed him the most.

It was easier to focus on his work than on the fear of being useless. Unfortunately, stuffing his bag full of gauze wasn't exactly a task that kept his mind away from what was happening around him.

The fight was coming, and they wouldn't all make it out alive.

Gideon had known he'd find Lisha in the infirmary, so as soon as his meeting was over, that was where he headed. He found him standing in front of one of the beds, pushing things into the bag he carried around when he visited patients. He was pale and looked almost in a trance, as if his thoughts were stuck on something only he could see.

Gideon could too easily imagine what Lisha was thinking about. He'd been thinking about the same things nonstop and wasn't quite sure how to deal with those thoughts. He'd never expected to find himself face to face with a fight to the death, and what he might see terrified him. He could only imagine what Lisha felt like.

He was a healer, but he'd never had to deal with the kind

of wounds and horror he would see on the battlefield. Even worse, some of the people he might have to take care of would be his friends. Could Lisha really deal with that kind of situation? Gideon didn't know, and it wasn't his place to question Lisha. Lisha was doing what he knew best, which was taking care of people. He'd do so even if it destroyed him, and Gideon knew that if he tried to talk him out of doing this, Lisha would tell him to fuck off, although probably not in those words. Lisha was the head healer at the palace. He was the one in charge of the other healers, which would have qualified him to stay back. That wasn't how Lisha was, though. If there was a fight where people could be hurt, he'd be in the middle of it, saving as many people as he could as the battle raged around him.

It was really fucking terrifying, and Gideon had no idea how to deal with it or even if he could. It was better to ignore it until they couldn't anymore. Thankfully, that wouldn't be tonight.

"It's time to leave," he told Lisha.

Lisha gave him the stink eye. "Good evening to you, too," he grumbled.

Gideon grinned. "Good evening. How was your day, my love?"

Lisha's cheeks darkened, but he looked pleased. He always did when Gideon talked to him like that.

Gideon needed to do it more often.

"It's been a day," Lisha said with a sigh. "We handed over the egg, which was the right thing to do, but it was also hard."

"Because you'd come to care for it."

"Both Christian and I have. We know it's for the best, though."

"The baby will be safe with the Eiloren clan, and I'm sure they'll allow you to visit if you want. Even if you don't, you can get news about the baby by phone. They won't keep the child from you if you want to check in on them."

"But it's not my job anymore."

"So? You don't have to check in on them as a healer. You can do it as someone who was worried about them and wants the best for them." Gideon grinned. "Just like I want the best for you, and right now, that means putting away everything and going to dinner."

Lisha glared, but his stomach growled at the same time, which lessened the effect. Lisha rolled his eyes when Gideon snickered, then, thankfully, put his bag down. "I'm ready whenever you want to go," he said. "It's time to get out of this infirmary."

"We can go now."

"Who's going to be there tonight?" Lisha asked as they left the infirmary.

Gideon felt better now that he'd gotten Lisha away. He'd be back early tomorrow, but the evening was for them.

"It would be easier to ask who isn't going to be there." Gideon paused and frowned. "Actually, I think everyone will be there."

Lisha groaned. "That's going to be messy."

It would be, but Gideon knew it pleased Lisha.

For so long, he'd been a loner. He'd told Gideon that, and Gideon had heard from his voice that it had hurt him. Lisha had explained it was because he'd studied for years, then he'd needed some time to learn a new life where he was a healer, then the head healer. The past few decades had been a whirlwind for him, and family and friends had been placed on the back burner.

As had Lisha's love life, but that was over now, as was the rest. He had friends and family, and it was time for him to spend time with them. Hopefully, they'd have plenty of opportunities to do so once the war was over.

Even though Gideon didn't want to think about the war

and what might happen, he couldn't avoid doing so and wasn't the only one. Everyone at dinner was worried, and there was tension between them, but Gideon didn't know how to fix any of that. He didn't think anyone knew how to deal with an upcoming war and the knowledge that some of the people around their table might not make it. Gideon desperately wanted to do something about it, but what? There was nothing more he could do. If he had the possibility, he'd wrap everyone in one of those plastic sheets with the bubbles, even though it would make it hard for the dragons to shift. He didn't care.

He only cared that the people here tonight were his family and that they needed to be all right. Unfortunately, he couldn't protect all of them. He couldn't even protect Lisha. He wasn't a fighter, and he hoped that wouldn't come back to bite him in the ass.

But even if it did, he'd been happy. He had family and friends, and he'd made the most out of the time he had with them since he'd arrived at the palace.

He had to think positively. It didn't matter that all of them were terrified and worried. The fight would end in just a few days, and everyone would meet around the table again.

Gideon wouldn't have it any other way.

CHAPTER TEN

The tension in the palace was so thick that Gideon could have sworn he could touch it with a finger if he tried. Everyone was on edge, and it was creating problems, which he didn't need any more of.

So when he heard a group of human soldiers grumbling about having to live with dragons and worrying they might get eaten, he'd decided to step in before things could degenerate into a fight. He understood where they were coming from, even though he'd never felt that way, even when he'd first arrived at the palace. He'd never been afraid of dragons. He'd had a healthy respect for them when he'd believed they were animals, but as soon as he'd realized they had a human part, he'd been ecstatic at the thought of talking to them.

He hadn't been disappointed. Even with the war looming at their doorstep, he still thought this was the best job ever. He could see why the soldiers were nervous, though. They had a different point of view. To them, the dragons were massive killing machines, and whether or not they'd ever seen a dragon attack or kill humans, their imaginations were probably as good as Gideon's in that aspect.

The soldiers were tucked in an alcove by a window, talking not as quietly as they clearly thought. Gideon had heard them from where he'd been walking down the hallway that intersected with the one they were in, so he'd turned the corner. He could now see them, and he straightened his back and raised his chin.

Then he cleared his throat.

Four soldiers were leaning together, and they all jumped apart as if he'd caught them doing something illegal. They lined up before him when they realized who he was, but he didn't want that. He wasn't their superior.

"It's fine," he told them, waving at them to relax. "But I happened to hear your conversation."

They looked at each other. Gideon leaned closer to see their names, but he didn't want their surnames. He wasn't their friend, but he did want them to see him as a friendly person and someone they could come to if they needed to talk about their lives with the dragons.

"We're sorry, sir," one of the men said.

Gideon wouldn't get them to stop calling him sir, so he didn't try. "What's your name? Actually, what are all your names?"

The man looked at the others, then back at Gideon. "I'm Josh. These are Zachary, Leroy, and Sam."

"It's a pleasure to meet you all. As I said, I heard that you're wary of the dragons."

"They're . . . big," Sam said.

"They are. They're also scary in both their forms. Their dragons are formidable and have wicked claws and fangs. Even in their human forms, they look alien to us."

"But you're comfortable living here," Josh said.

"I am. I'm not afraid of them, and I've never been."

"How? It would be so easy for them to eat you in one bite."

"And it would be easy for you to shoot me, yet you won't. Why not?"

"I don't have a reason to."

"Exactly. They might not be human, but it doesn't mean they don't reason like us. Why would any of the Ogorth clan members want to hurt you? Even those who don't like the thought of humans living at the palace and helping with the war know better. Hurting any of you would take the government's support from the clan, and they need it. More importantly, they respect life, be it human or dragon. As long as you don't give them a reason to attack you, they won't. Treat them like you would any other ally."

"Humans haven't been good to dragons in the past," Sam murmured.

"We haven't, but they'll give you the benefit of the doubt. They know not every human hunted them. They know you're here to help them. They want the same things we want. They want families and to be safe and happy. Attacking any of you, especially when you're guests of the queen, would mean losing all of that, and I doubt anyone here wants that."

Gideon wasn't sure he'd convinced the group, but he'd done his best and thought a few had relaxed. He didn't expect them to become best friends with dragons and skip down the hallways hand in hand with them, but that wasn't what he'd been aiming for. He just wanted dragons and soldiers to respect each other and to work together. Even if this was his only contribution to the war, he'd see it as a good one if he was able to change even one mind.

The day had finally come. Well, it hadn't come yet, but it would tomorrow, which meant Lisha was all over the place. Everything was ready, but he still found himself going over all of it again.

Twice.

He was nervous and terrified. He was scared of being in the middle of the fight, of something happening to him, and of something happening to Gideon. He was scared for his friends and the clan. He didn't know what would happen, but even if everything went in favor of the Ogorth clan, there would still be wounded dragons and deaths. Lisha wasn't sure how to deal with that, which was why he'd been fussing over details the entire morning. He needed to be distracted, but Gideon was the only person who could do that. The problem was that Gideon had work to do, and Lisha didn't want to bother him.

On the other hand, if something were to happen to either of them tomorrow, he wanted to spend the day with Gideon. What was he supposed to do?

"You've already checked your bag five times this morning," Neena said.

She was sitting by the window, sipping on a cup of tea. Lisha glared at her, but she didn't seem offended. She was right not to be, and she was right that he'd already checked his bag five times today. There was nothing else he could add to it, but the things he'd be carrying during the fight didn't feel like enough.

They were emergency supplies, just enough to stabilize as many people as possible before they could be transported to the palace. Once they were here, Neena and the others would take care of them. The human doctors who'd arrived with the soldiers would be in the infirmary, too, and while they weren't experts in dragon anatomy, Lisha had told them enough that they'd be able to help anyone, not just humans. Their anatomy wasn't so different that they wouldn't be capable of saving the dragons who needed it.

The work tomorrow would be divided between the infirmary and the landing pad. The Ogorth clan healers would be working with healers from other clans, and they needed people upstairs in case dragons were brought in unable to shift back to their human form. It would complicate things, but they would be fighting as dragons. They wouldn't shift back if they were unconscious, but they'd still need medical attention. That was why Lisha had spent the past week organizing an emergency infirmary on the roof. Between that and the infirmary in the palace, there should be enough space for everyone who needed it.

They wouldn't help anyone if the Saganto clan won, but that wasn't something Lisha was willing to consider. He couldn't because if he did, he'd start panicking, and that was the last thing he needed.

He put down his bag and closed his eyes. There were better ways for him to spend this day, but he didn't know how he could do it. He was pretty sure that if he tried walking away from the infirmary, he'd feel guilty because he wasn't working. At the same time, he felt guilty because he was working instead of spending time with Gideon.

What was he supposed to do?

He heard Neena move, and when he opened his eyes, she stood before him. She squeezed his shoulder, and Lisha could see the fear he felt reflected in her expression. He wasn't the only one risking his life. He wasn't the only one who would have people he loved out there tomorrow and who was terrified of losing them. Everyone was in the same boat, and everyone knew how he felt.

That didn't feel any less overwhelming.

On instinct, he grabbed Neena and pulled her into his arms. He didn't think they'd ever hugged, but after a squeak of surprise, she wrapped her arms around his waist and held him close. For a moment, they stood there, taking comfort in each other. Lisha wanted to promise everything would be all right, but he had no way of knowing if that would be true, and he didn't want to lie. Besides, Neena knew as well as he did that everything would not be all right.

"You should go to Gideon," she murmured as she stepped back.

"Someone has to stay in the infirmary." Because even though the big fight would happen tomorrow, today, there were still kids with tummy aches and people who hurt themselves in accidents.

"The doctors can stay. It'll do them good to deal with dragon patients for the rest of the day, but since we'll be around the palace, they can still call us if they have a problem. A few already volunteered so we could go home, and I think we should accept their offer."

It was just a question of deciding what Lisha wanted to feel guilty about, but it didn't take long. If this was his last day on earth, he wanted to spend it with Gideon. If anyone needed him, they knew where to find him. In the meantime, he'd be with the man he loved.

After checking in with the doctors, he and Neena left the infirmary. Gideon was no doubt in his office so that was where Lisha headed. He crossed paths with several dragons, and everyone seemed as tense as he felt. The entire palace felt that way, which wasn't a surprise, but Lisha couldn't wait until it was over. This was his home, and he wanted to be comfortable in it. He wanted to be happy and safe, and the only reason he wasn't was the Saganto clan.

He didn't think he'd ever despised anyone the way he despised their leader. He was doing all of this because he was power-hungry and cruel, and it wasn't something Lisha could understand. He'd tried to put himself in Sigmund's place, but he truly couldn't wrap his mind around it. It could only be because he wanted more power, but what would he do with it? Was he really planning on attacking the human world once he was done destroying the dragon world? That felt like a stupid idea.

The human government was allied with the Ogorth clan, which was a good thing. There were so many more humans than dragons, and even though a dragon could easily kill a human or even a small group of humans, once there were more of them, especially using the weapons Lisha had seen on some of the soldiers who now lived at the palace, the dragon would die. Of course, the Saganto clan leader didn't care how many dragons were killed. He wanted power and to win, and he was ready to sacrifice a lot to obtain that.

Lisha didn't think he'd ever understand that. He didn't *want* to understand it, because if he did, he feared it would make him too similar to Sigmund. After everything he'd seen lately, the thought made him shudder in horror.

The reason behind what the Saganto clan was doing didn't matter, anyway. What did matter was their actions and results, and those were horrible. Dragons were dying. Even when they didn't die from their wounds, they were scarred and changed for the rest of their lives. Lisha would never forgive the Saganto clan for this, and while he had no doubt they didn't care about how he felt about them, they'd made an enemy out of most of the dragon world.

The dragons had survived because they'd ignored each other for a long time, then because they'd decided to build alliances. The Saganto clan was alone, and while they were strong and numerous, they wouldn't be forever. They were losing dragons, and they would lose even more tomorrow.

Because the Ogorth clan would win. Lisha was sure of that and didn't want to think about the possibility of them losing. He couldn't afford to do so, so he didn't.

Instead, he headed to Gideon's office and knocked on his door.

"Come in," Gideon called out when he heard the knock.

It wasn't Jennifer, because she didn't usually wait after knocking, but whoever was there had her approval, because otherwise they wouldn't be knocking. She was a great assistant, and Gideon had found himself thanking her for taking the job more than once. The last time he had, she'd told him to shut up and do his job.

He had, because she was a little scary when she got

annoyed.

The door opened, and Lisha appeared. Gideon instantly put down the pen he'd been using to tap a rhythm on his desk and got up from his chair. He wasn't really working and was glad for the distraction.

He couldn't focus on anything today. He wasn't surprised, and after a while, he'd stopped trying. With the fight looming so close, how was anyone supposed to focus on anything?

He had a hard time believing that tomorrow at this time, the Ogorth clan would be at war. The sky would be filled with dragons, the ground with soldiers, and the world with blood. If Gideon didn't keep himself in check, he'd run away screaming, which was something he'd been trying very hard not to do.

No one expected him to be a fighter, but he did need to preserve some dignity. Showing people how scared he was wasn't a good idea, but this was Lisha. He already knew how scared Gideon was, and he shared that feeling. Gideon was pretty sure that everyone at the palace did, even those acting as if tomorrow's fight would be nothing more than a skirmish.

"I thought you'd be in the infirmary," Gideon murmured.

"I was, but I wasn't doing anything productive, and Neena told me to come here."

Gideon opened his arms, and Lisha snuggled right into them. For a moment they stood quietly, wrapped around each other. Gideon couldn't even think about the possibility that he might not have this anymore tomorrow.

Lisha wouldn't be in the thick of the fight, but he'd be under it. He'd be keeping an eye on the dragons in the air and running around saving and helping people who needed him. The problem was that he wouldn't be alone on the ground. It would be crawling with hunters, and while that was where the human soldiers came in, Gideon's brain could still imagine too many ways in which Lisha could get hurt. He was a dragon, but it wouldn't take much. Lisha wasn't a fighter. He was a healer, a caring dragon who never wanted anyone to be hurt.

Gideon was ready to deal with the consequences of what would happen tomorrow, with the nightmares and everything that would come with what Lisha would see, but if something happened to Lisha, he didn't know what he'd do. Once again, he was tempted to beg Lisha to stay at the palace, but he kept the words to himself. Lisha had made his decision, and it wouldn't be fair for Gideon to try to change his mind. Lisha might be the man he loved, but he was also a healer, and his place would be out there, helping his people.

"I hate all of this," Lisha said as he leaned back.

"I think we all hate it."

He pulled Lisha toward the sitting area by the window. He loved it because it was comfortable and informal, and here, he and Lisha could spend some time trying not to think about the fight. They couldn't ignore it completely, but for a moment, they could imagine that this was just another day in their life together.

They settled on the couch facing the window. The only thing Gideon could see from here was trees, and he loved it. It was like being lost in the middle of the forest, completely alone, or in this case, with Lisha. Sometimes he needed that feeling of being on his own. There were so many people at the palace, and he wasn't used to sharing his living space with so many others. Here in this office, Gideon could spend some time in silence and peace, and that was what they did.

They didn't need to talk. They both knew what the other felt, and they'd already promised they would both come back at the end of the fight tomorrow. Lisha would be careful, and he'd be protected, but the thought of him so close to the fight was still enough to give Gideon nightmares.

But there was no way out of this, and Gideon accepted it.

He wouldn't love Lisha if he were different, if he cared less about his clan and his people, if he were too afraid to do the right thing.

"It's almost over," he whispered.

Lisha snuggled closer to him, pressing his head against Gideon's chest. Gideon buried his nose into Lisha's hair, closing his eyes.

It *was* almost over. It had to be.

CHAPTER ELEVEN

Lisha stood on the landing pad, surrounded by nurses, other healers, and dragon fighters. They were taking the fight to the Saganto clan, which meant Lisha would have to shift and fly there. He wouldn't stay in the air for long, though. As soon as the fight started, he and the others would land, shift back, and be ready to tend to the wounded.

"Do we really have to fly?" one of the human soldiers asked.

He was blond with blue eyes, and his face looked slightly green.

Now probably wasn't the time for him to freak out about flying, but Lisha supposed it was better than freaking out about dying. "I'll carry you," he said.

The soldier was young, and Lisha didn't understand why he was here, risking his life for people he didn't know. Shouldn't he be at home with his parents? But just like Lisha had decided to go out there and be part of the fight, so had this man. It didn't matter how young he was. His actions were more important than his age.

"I'm sure you mean well, but it doesn't matter who I fly with. It's really freaking scary," the soldier said.

"Close your eyes and think that you're on one of these roller coaster things humans enjoy so much."

Lisha hadn't thought it possible, but the man's face turned even greener.

"I always get sick on roller coasters," he muttered.

There was nothing Lisha could do for him, so instead, he

focused on himself. He checked that he had everything he'd need one last time, then looked at the other healers doing the same. They all wore a similar bag hooked around their neck. The strap was long so that it could accommodate their dragon neck when they shifted. Once they shifted back, they could throw it over their shoulder, and it would be within reach when they needed something.

"Where's your boyfriend?" Orion asked.

He was Slavin's brother, so he was part of Lisha's group of friends. He'd be fighting, too, and Lisha had to remind himself not to think about what could happen to the many people he now considered family.

"We already said goodbye earlier," Lisha murmured.

Orion nodded. "We did the same."

One of Orion's partners, Dray, would be staying at the palace. He wasn't a fighter, so his place wouldn't be out here with the others. Orion's second partner was a guard, though, and Lisha couldn't imagine how they both felt. They hadn't been assigned to the same places, but that didn't mean they wouldn't see each other once they were in the air.

Lisha had been horrified by the fact that he wouldn't know what was happening to Gideon, but maybe it was a good thing. He could only imagine what would happen if he were there to see Gideon be attacked or worse. That was what Orion and Nithe were going through, and Lisha wished there was more he could do for them. Besides murmuring words of reassurance, though, there wasn't anything *anyone* could do for them.

A loud explosion in the distance made the floor under Lisha's feet shake. He gasped and reached for Orion, thankful when the other dragon kept him upright. Orion's expression was grim, and Lisha knew the time had come.

The battle had begun.

He was a healer, meaning he hadn't been among the first

to leave the palace. The human soldiers had left through the smaller doors at the base of the palace a while ago and were stalking the hunters in the forest. Numerous groups of dragons had flown away before, getting ready to attack the Saganto clan. It was still early, with the sun barely peeking at the horizon, but the time didn't matter when it came to fighting.

Orion looked around the group. "Ready?"

The humans were a bit more hesitant in their answers, but they wouldn't back down. The blond moved closer to Lisha, and he had to tell him to take a step back while he shifted. As he did so, he heard some of the soldiers gasp, and when he looked at the one he'd be transporting, he saw that the man was staring at him with wide eyes. He should have asked for his name, but it was too late now.

Lisha and the other healers and nurses wouldn't be using saddles. It would be too complicated for them to take them off when they wanted to shift back to human. That meant the humans would have to straddle them with no help, which wouldn't be easy for them. Still, they didn't hesitate, not even the queasy blond. He scrambled up Lisha's back, and when he squeezed his knees around Lisha, Lisha knew he was ready.

He opened his wings. It had been a while since he'd flown. Most of the dragons had stayed inside the palace because everyone had been too afraid that the Saganto clan would attack. It felt good to push on his legs and get into the air again after so long, and he wished it wasn't under these circumstances. He wanted to take Gideon flying. He wanted to take him to his favorite places, to show him the world as he knew it, and hopefully, once the day was over, he'd be able to do so.

But first, they had to fight.

He rose in the air, careful of the dragons around him. He and the other healers were surrounded by guards so that they wouldn't be attacked on their way to the fight. They needed to get there in one piece because otherwise, they would be of no use to the guards already fighting.

They headed in the direction from which the explosion had come from. Lisha had been told that the Saganto clan had been hiding in the forest, gathering people and getting ready to attack. They'd planned on doing so tonight once the Ogorth clan had fallen asleep. Instead, they'd gotten the surprise of their lives because the Ogorth clan had attacked first.

Lisha felt savage satisfaction that they were finally acting. The Saganto clan had been allowed to do what they wanted for too long, and that time was finally over. Lisha wasn't normally so bloodthirsty, but he'd seen too many people hurt his clan. He wanted revenge, even though it wasn't a healer's way of feeling.

As they flew away from the palace and safety, Lisha looked down. He hadn't expected to be able to see the fights on the ground, so he was surprised when he did. It was easy to recognize the humans on his side, since they all wore uniforms, and from what he was able to tell, they seemed to be winning. He saw too many bodies to count, so he didn't try. Instead, he focused on the fact that most of those bodies weren't wearing uniforms.

As they neared the battlefield, his stomach churned. He could see dragons fighting in the distance, their wings fluttering around each other as they used them to fly and fight. Most of the fights were a whirlwind of claws, wings, and fangs, and Lisha was afraid to get too close. Luckily for him, he didn't have to reach the middle of the fight. Instead, once they were close enough, Orion guided their group toward the ground. They landed, the ground shaking under their feet, and as soon as the soldier slid from Lisha's back, Lisha shifted. He twisted his bag to his side so it wouldn't bother him, but then there was nothing for him to do.

Yet.

He looked up at the sky again. He felt horrible, waiting here for someone to get hurt. He hoped no one did, but this was a war. People *were* going to get hurt. They were going to die.

Lisha was here to help every single one of them.

The blond soldier he'd transported sucked in a breath. Lisha wasn't surprised to see he was staring up. He was supposed to protect Lisha and the others, though, so after giving him a few seconds, Lisha cleared his throat.

The soldier's cheeks flushed. He didn't say anything, but he didn't have to. Lisha understood how he felt.

He'd never seen this kind of fight before, and it was impressive in a grim way. He still couldn't allow himself to be distracted. He might not be fighting for his life right now, but the dragons in the air were, and he was there for them.

Even though it had happened away from the palace, Gideon had felt the explosion. As soon as the floor under him had shaken, he'd rushed to the window, looking in the distance. The explosion had been the signal for the start of the fight, and even though he had to squint to be able to see something, the fight in the distance was obvious.

"Is it weird that I'm glad they're so far away?" Sheldon muttered next to him.

He was looking out the window, too. Gideon imagined he was looking for Morven and that, at the same time, he was terrified to see something happening to the man he loved.

"I don't think it's weird," Gideon told him. "I think it's the way you're dealing with it, and that's perfectly fine."

Sheldon nodded and pulled his attention away from the window for a moment to look at his daughter. They'd gathered all the children of the palace and their parents if they weren't involved in the fighting. They hadn't stayed in the nursery, though. That would be the first place someone would look if they searched for the children. Instead, they'd all gathered in a guest suite, and while it was crowded, Gideon was glad he wasn't alone. He didn't know what he would have done if he hadn't had the support of his friends, and he was pretty sure they felt the same way.

The children didn't seem to realize something was happening, but most of them were too young to notice anything. That was a good thing. They wouldn't be traumatized by the war, although Gideon couldn't imagine what would happen if one of them were to lose a parent.

He told himself not to think about that. He couldn't afford to if he didn't want to freak out. He was the only one here who wasn't responsible for a particular child, but he felt responsible for the entire group. He wasn't a soldier or a dragon guard, and they were safe in this suite, but that didn't mean he wasn't keeping an eye out.

That was why he noticed the two dragons flying toward the castle. Initially, they were little more than pinpricks in the distance. He didn't think much of it until the pinpricks grew and became dragons.

The problem was that he couldn't identify them. He had no idea what he was looking at, and it made him nervous.

It could be two of their dragons coming back to the palace, but if so, why were they flying straight for the side of the mountain rather than for the landing pad? Not all the guards had left the palace. If these dragons were enemies, the Ogorth clan would eliminate them. There was nothing Gideon could do against a dragon, let alone two, so he looked down at the fight at their feet instead. They'd been warned by one of the queen's spies that while the Saganto clan had kept their distance, they'd sent the human hunters ahead. Humans had an easier time hiding in the forest, so if the Ogorth clan hadn't known about them, they would have been able to attack without anyone stopping them.

This fight was even more difficult to see. Unless he focused, he could only see trees. He knew the soldiers were fighting the hunters, but beyond seeing a man here and there, the only thing telling him what was happening was the sound of guns.

And screaming.

"What's that?" Sheldon asked, leaning so close to the window that his nose brushed against it.

"Dragons," Gideon said.

Sheldon turned to him. "Enemies?"

"I don't know, but they're making me uncomfortable."

Sheldon nodded. "Why aren't they going to the landing pad?"

Gideon was glad he wasn't the only one wondering that. It meant he wasn't going nuts like he'd thought and hoped. He would have rather seen things than have two enemies headed straight for them.

But that was what was happening. There was no way these dragons knew where the babies were, but that didn't mean they weren't here for them. More likely, they were here to find and kill the queen and the Eiloren king, as well as the other leaders who had gathered in the throne room. Gideon had been invited to spend the battle with them, but he'd decided to be with his family instead.

He looked back at the room. All the humans were here, but also many dragons who would fight to the death to protect their families. Gideon couldn't ask that of them, but he was pretty sure he wouldn't have to. They would all shift and protect their people if it came to that.

He turned his attention back to the window. The dragons were still coming. They were so close that he could see their colors. One was a bright green, while the other was a muddy red, almost the color of blood.

Another two dragons appeared. They were coming from the landing pad, so Gideon was sure they were on their side. They rushed the dragons approaching, and Gideon sucked in a breath when they clashed in a tangle of wings and claws.

He couldn't look away from the fight, yet at the same time, he desperately wanted to. He didn't want to see these dragons tearing each other apart. He didn't want to see blood and wounds and death.

He looked away. His stomach churned, and for a moment, he thought he might be about to throw up. He didn't think anyone in the room would care or say anything about it, but he breathed in and out a few times, telling himself everything would be all right.

He'd almost convinced himself it would, but then Sheldon sucked in a breath. Gideon quickly turned, just in time to see one of the Ogorth dragons plummet to the ground. The other one was still fighting the second enemy dragon, but now that they were free, the first Saganto dragon turned their attention back to the palace.

"This isn't good," Gideon said.

"What do we do?" Sheldon asked.

Gideon didn't have an answer. He had no idea what this dragon was planning. Even if they attacked the palace, the windows were too small for any dragon to fit through. They could shift and try to fit in that way, but they'd be putting themselves in danger of falling to their death.

The only entrance where a dragon would fit was the landing pad, but that was where everyone was waiting for an attack. There was no way this dragon would be allowed into the palace, and they had to know that.

What was the Saganto dragon doing, then? What was their plan? They had to be following the orders of their leader, but Gideon didn't understand what the goal was. The Saganto dragon couldn't attack the palace alone or even with another dragon. They couldn't get into the palace to the queen. But they could act as a distraction.

CHAPTER TWELVE

Lisha pulled on the claw stuck in the dragon's thigh. The dragon bellowed, the sound loud even over the fight above their heads. Lisha ignored all of it and used his arm to wipe the sweat from his forehead. The claw was still stuck, and he couldn't get it out.

He looked sideways at the nurse. "I think we're going to have to move them like this," he said.

Her eyes were wide. "I don't think we can."

"I don't know if we have a choice."

Lisha glared down at the claw. The dragon in which it was stuck flopped against the earth, a small cloud of dust wrapping around them. Their skin was clammy and cold, and Lisha wasn't even done yet. He'd already taken out three claws from the dragon's thigh, and he still had one left.

He had no idea how this had happened. An entire paw had been stuck in the dragon's leg. It looked like something had torn it from the dragon it had belonged to while they'd been attacking the wounded dragon. Lisha supposed he should be relieved it wasn't still attached to the attacker, but it didn't solve all his problems.

He sucked in a breath, wrapped his fingers around the claw, and pulled again.

The dragon screamed. Lisha had to work hard to ignore the sound, and he told himself that he was only trying to help. The dragon knew that. They were doing their best not to snap at Lisha, but it couldn't be easy. They were in pain and bleeding, and while the wound wasn't lethal, it could become so. It could get infected, especially if Lisha couldn't remove the claw. If he was unable to do so, he'd have to wait until they were in the infirmary with his knives and sterile environment.

The claw moved, and Lisha hissed. He continued pulling, doing his best not to make the wound worse but at the same time putting all his force into it.

The claw came out with a horrible sucking sound. Lisha threw it aside and rushed to help the dragon, the nurse handing things over as he worked. He quickly cleaned the wounds, checked that there was no debris in any of them, and bandaged them as well as he could. That would be enough until the dragon reached the palace. There, the other healers would take care of them.

Eventually, Lisha stepped back and nodded at the guards closest to him. "They can be evacuated."

The guard nodded back and went to work, and Lisha took a second to breathe.

He didn't know how many dragons he'd saved today. He'd lost count after tending to his tenth one and refused to continue counting. He didn't need proof of what the Saganto clan was doing. He was in the middle of the fight, surrounded by blood and war, unable to avoid them.

He shivered and looked around to make sure no one needed him. The fight was still raging above his head, and he was afraid to look up.

That was what saved him.

Since he wasn't looking up, he noticed something rustling in the bushes. He tensed, but he expected an animal. What he got was a human hunter throwing himself out of the bushes, raising a knife high above his head. The man screamed, and Lisha screamed back, unsure what to do. He stumbled, and the only thing he could think of was that this hunter was about to kill him.

Luckily for him, he wasn't alone. He was surrounded by

soldiers and dragons, and several of them sprang into action as Lisha put as much distance as possible between himself and the hunter.

Someone grabbed Lisha's shoulder and pulled while someone else stepped in front of him. Seconds later, the hunter's body hit the ground. The cloud of dust wasn't as impressive as it had been earlier, but Lisha couldn't look away.

There was so much blood. Lisha could smell it, but he was pretty sure that the blood he smelled didn't belong to the hunter. It was all around him, so much more blood than he was used to or knew how to deal with.

"Are you okay?" the dragon who'd stepped in front of Lisha asked, turning to him.

The dragon dismissed the hunter's body, but Lisha couldn't look away. He had to force himself to do so, and when he did, it was to meet a pair of dark blue eyes heavy with worry. He didn't understand why, because he didn't know this dragon, but it felt good to know that he was safe.

He nodded, trying to find his voice. "He didn't touch me," he eventually croaked.

The blue dragon nodded again. "Good. My king would have my head if I let anything happen to the queen's healer."

Lisha had thought this dragon didn't belong to the Ogorth clan because he didn't recognize him, but he hadn't known which clan he belonged to because the symbol on his shoulder was half covered in blood. Now, he suspected it was Killian's clan. There were other dragons here, some of them following a queen, others a king, but from the way this dragon talked, it was clear his king was close to Lisha's queen.

"Thank you. I'm Lisha, and if you need anything, you just have to ask."

The dragon grinned. "Well, I hope never to need your services. I'm Elodio, and we should probably move."

He was right. It was bad enough that Lisha was a target

when he was taking care of the fallen warriors because he couldn't move. He shouldn't stay still when he wasn't busy taking care of open wounds and broken limbs. He should make it harder for the Saganto clan to hurt him.

An explosion rocked Lisha's world. He reached out, but there was nothing for him to catch to stay on his feet. Elodio seemed to realize that and grabbed Lisha's shoulder, keeping both of them upright as the world shook under their feet. Lisha looked around, needing to know what was happening. The explosion didn't sound like it had happened close by, and they were right under the fight. If this wasn't the clans attacking each other, what was it?

Lisha's gaze drifted into the distance, where the palace stood.

Or rather, where it had stood before. Lisha could only see a thick cloud of dark smoke rising toward the sky. It wrapped around part of the palace, and it was impossible for anyone to tell if the palace and the mountain were still standing.

It would take a lot to bring down the Ogorth clan palace, but it wouldn't be impossible, especially if someone was as bent on revenge like the Saganto clan leader. Lisha wanted to scream, but fear gripped his throat. Gideon was at the palace. The rest of Lisha's family was there, too, including the children and his queen, but he was here, so far away that there was nothing he could do.

As soon as the world stopped shaking, Lisha started running. He ignored the people screaming for him to stop. He couldn't get to the palace on foot, which meant he needed to shift and fly. In turn, that meant he needed to leave the area, because if he tried flying from here, he'd be right in the middle of the fight, which wasn't something he could deal with. Not only was Gideon in danger, but Lisha wasn't a fighter, and it would be too easy for the dragons fighting to grab and hurt him.

"We need a healer," someone yelled.

Lisha stumbled. He was close to the voice, which meant he could be useful, but the palace was burning. Gideon was there, possibly hurt, and Lisha couldn't help him. The only thing he wanted to do was to run to Gideon.

But that wasn't his place.

His place was here, in the fight, helping his clan win the war. Gideon would be pissed if Lisha reached him only for him to be perfectly fine. Lisha was sure other dragons were already flying back to the palace to take care of whatever had happened. They'd know what to do, but he wouldn't, and he'd probably be more of a problem than a solution. Here, though, he could make a difference.

So even though his heart was being torn apart, he turned away from the palace and toward the dragon who needed him.

For a moment, the only thing Gideon could hear was loud buzzing. It took him a second to realize that the explosion had been so loud that his ears still hadn't recovered. He didn't need them to, though. What he needed to do was to start moving.

Thankfully, the explosion hadn't involved the part of the palace where he and the others were, but it had been close. He wasn't sure what happened, but he'd seen the one Saganto dragon who'd managed to escape rush toward the side of the mountain. Something had been strapped to their stomach, and Gideon had barely had time to wonder what that was before the world exploded around him.

"They had a bomb," someone whispered next to him.

He turned to Sheldon, who was trying to get to his feet. Gideon scrambled to help him, but Sheldon barely looked at him. Instead, he turned toward the back of the room, frantically looking for something. Gideon realized that Sheldon was looking for his daughter, so he wasn't surprised when he rushed away as soon as he saw her.

Gideon had many people he wanted to check on, but the only ones he could check on were all in this room. They could take care of each other while Gideon tried to find out what happened.

He moved to the door, quietly opening it to peek into the hallway. He sucked in a breath when he saw the hole in the palace wall. The hallway was open to the sky, and through the hole, Gideon could see several more dragons coming closer.

They had to be from the Saganto clan. The first two dragons had been sent to poke holes into the mountain, and these would sneak in and take the Ogorth clan from the inside.

Gideon swallowed. He couldn't allow that to happen. He wasn't sure what he could do to prevent it, but it seemed like he and the others were stuck. They wouldn't have time to run.

"What's going on?" one of the guards who'd stayed behind asked, trying to push past Gideon out of the room.

Gideon held him back. "What's going on is that there's a freaking hole in the palace and dragons headed for it."

The guard's eyes widened. "Saganto clan?"

"They have to be. We need to lock this door."

The guard nodded. He probably knew what he was doing better than Gideon, so for a moment, Gideon felt better. He wouldn't have to take charge. He wouldn't have to be the one to save the people in this room.

Then something pushed hard against the hold he had on the door. He stumbled back, but he wasn't giving up yet. He pushed the door, even though he knew he wouldn't be able to close it. The room behind him had fallen eerily silent, and he hoped they were getting out through the other door. It had been a good idea to get everyone into a room with more than one exit, and while Gideon was stuck here, he didn't mind.

He minded because he didn't want to die, but if this was what it took to save Sheldon, the babies, and everyone else, he'd die knowing he'd done a good thing.

But he'd really rather not die.

He turned to the guard as he continued pushing back against the door. "Get everyone out," he snapped.

The guard jumped into action. Gideon didn't dare turn around to look at what was happening, but then he realized it would be easier for him to keep these dragons out if he did. He pressed his back against the door and pushed with his feet, putting his entire weight and strength into it. There were still too many people in the room, dammit.

Gideon wasn't sure how he managed to keep this up. He wasn't a gym guy, and he was pretty sure one of the babies could easily beat him in a fight. Still, he managed to stay where he was, keeping the dragons out until only one person was left in the room with him. The guard looked at Gideon, probably wondering how he was supposed to get him away from the door without it opening and dragons streaming through.

Gideon swallowed. He hadn't expected to sacrifice himself, but he was doing it for a good reason and for people he cared about. At least, he'd die knowing that.

"Lock the door behind yourself," he ordered.

The guard's eyes were wide, but he nodded. The problem was that he was pushed aside. Gideon glared at Jacob.

"Go with him."

"No. Our job is to protect you."

The guard looked from Jacob, Nate, and Edgar to Gideon, clearly not knowing what to do. Gideon didn't know how to convince them to leave, but he had to.

"I know what your job is, and I'm grateful to have you here, but think about it. I'm just a guy. I can and will be replaced if something happens to me. Those kids in the other room, though? They're the future of the Ogorth clan and of the alliance between dragons and humans. They need to be protected more than I do, and I trust the three of you to do it. Please."

Gideon expected at least one of them to argue. He wasn't surprised when Edgar slipped away almost instantly, but Nate hesitated before doing the same. Jacob looked pissed, though. His jaw was set, and Gideon was sure he'd decided stay.

He didn't get the opportunity. The guard pushed Jacob through the escape door, taking him by surprise. Gideon heard Jacob yell, but the door slammed shut, cutting his voice off. The sound of the door closing and locking was final, and for a moment, Gideon thought he might start crying. He had no intention of dying if he could avoid it, though. The push against his back was becoming stronger, and he needed to do something.

"I'll come out," he screamed through the door.

"You'll come out whether you like it or not," a dragon growled from the hallway.

That didn't sound good. "Just let the others go, all right?"

There was a pause, then another voice. "You'll come out without running if we promise we won't hurt them?"

"Yes."

"All right. Open the door."

Gideon only had a few seconds to move. He had no plan in mind, but he couldn't stay behind the door, and he definitely couldn't open it because he didn't believe any promise coming from a Saganto clan member. The door from which the others had run was locked, which only left the closet.

Gideon moved faster than he ever knew he could. As soon as the push against his back stopped, he rushed toward the closet. He'd checked it before, so he knew it was more like a small room than a closet where someone kept their clothing. It had a heavy lock on its door, too, and he almost cried when he saw the key was in it.

He slammed the door shut as the one he'd been leaning against slammed open, hitting the stone wall. He scrambled to lock the door, thankful it was made of heavy wood and a modern lock. He didn't know if it would be enough to keep however many dragons were out there away from him, but it would give him time.

That was all he needed. More guards would be coming. Blue was here, so the queen would have sent someone to look for him as soon as the explosion had happened.

The problem was that Gideon wasn't with the children. No one knew he was in this closet, which meant they wouldn't be looking for him.

He glanced around. There were a few pieces of discarded furniture in the room. He pushed everything in front of the door, but there were no windows or other entrances. Gideon had trapped himself, which meant he'd die if the Saganto clan dragons managed to get through.

He stared at the door. So far, no one had tried coming in, but it wouldn't last for long. He could hear dragons talking, and several sounded pissed, probably because he'd promised he'd come out and they'd thought they'd have an easy job getting their hands on the queen's child.

But Blue wasn't here, while Gideon was. He wouldn't be surprised if the Saganto dragons took it out on him once they got him out of this room.

He'd known he might die when the battle had started. He prayed he wouldn't, because he had too much to live for, but it was a distinct possibility at the moment. He knew everyone at the palace would have felt the explosion, and the sound had been loud enough to reach the battlefield. Hopefully, it meant dragons were coming back to help, although that might be a problem depending on how many of them the Saganto dragons had already taken out. Gideon wouldn't find out what was happening while he was stuck in this room, but there was nothing he could do about it. There was nothing he could do about his impending death, either.

He'd never been a praying man, but as he pressed his back against the wall and waited for the Saganto dragons to bust in, he prayed that both he and Lisha would be all right.

CHAPTER THIRTEEN

When Lisha had decided to stay behind, he'd known it would be hell. He'd been trying to move toward the palace as he helped dragons, but it was slow going when he had to stop every five minutes. His hands were slick with blood, he was exhausted, and he was more worried than he had ever been.

The smoke had dissipated, but unfortunately, that meant that Lisha could see the damage to the palace. Part of it was open to the elements, and he'd seen Saganto dragons sneaking in through the opening. They were inside the castle where Gideon was, where everyone Lisha cared about was. On the other hand, Lisha was down here, and while he was doing the right thing, it didn't mean he wasn't angry and terrified.

He wanted to find Gideon. He wanted to make sure he was all right and that none of those dragons had hurt him. He didn't know what he would do if he found Gideon wounded or worse. He didn't want to consider that possibility, but it was almost impossible.

"Watch out!" someone yelled.

Lisha looked up in time to see a dragon plummet to the ground. Their big body crashed into the trees, taking at least two down. It was hard to understand who this dragon belonged to, but it didn't really matter. Lisha had been trying to help every wounded dragon, and while he'd prioritized the Ogorth clan and their allies, he wasn't going to ignore the wounded Saganto clan members. He was a healer, and his job was to heal people, no matter who they were and what they'd done. Ignoring them could mean their death, and it would be on Lisha's head if that were to happen.

The ground shook when the dragon's body hit it, and Lisha rushed in that direction. Two of the nurses followed him, but they were flagging, and so was Lisha. He had no idea how long they'd been working and didn't care to find out. It felt like only a few seconds and an eternity at the same time, and the thought made his head hurt.

It was too late. When they reached the dragon, Lisha instantly saw they had a broken neck. He still checked for a pulse, relieved when he couldn't see any of the symbols that this dragon belonged to his clan or one of their allies on the dragon's skin. Everyone from the Ogorth clan and the clans they were working with had painted symbols on their bodies so they'd be identifiable. There was nothing like that here, and while Lisha still hated to see a life end, at least it wasn't someone on their side. He didn't know anything about this dragon, about why they were trying to destroy the Ogorth clan, but they may not have wanted to be there. Lisha would never know, but he wanted to give the dragon the benefit of the doubt. He wanted to believe they'd been forced to fight, so he did.

"There's nothing to be done here," he told the nurses as he stepped away.

He looked around. He didn't know how many people he'd helped since the fight had started, but it still didn't feel like enough. Lisha needed the battle to stop, dammit. He needed his people to be safe, not fighting for their lives.

He desperately wanted to run toward the palace and find Gideon. He still didn't know what had happened over there because no one had returned, but it was too easy to imagine. He could see the Saganto clan dragons rushing into the palace, even at a distance. Thankfully, he wasn't the only one, and more and more dragons were flying back to help. There weren't that many Saganto dragons left in the air battle, and Lisha prayed it meant the fight was almost over and not that they were all inside the palace.

For the war to truly be over, they needed to get the Saganto clan dragons out of the palace. That wasn't something Lisha could participate in, so instead, he did the next best thing.

He continued walking toward the palace, stopping every time he was needed. He cleaned and bandaged wounds, reassured wounded dragons, and set broken limbs. The entire time, he couldn't stop thinking about Gideon. Even helping people wasn't enough to distract him from the fear that something had happened to the man he loved, but he persisted.

Gideon loved him for who he was, and he wouldn't be himself if he didn't stop to help every dragon he could. If something had happened to Gideon, Lisha wanted to honor him like this.

And if nothing had happened to him and he was perfectly fine, they'd see each other at the palace as soon as Lisha was back.

Gideon knew his time had come when the door splintered, and the furniture against it jumped forward. He huddled against the back wall, but there was nowhere to hide or run. If he was getting out of here, he was pretty sure it would be feet first.

Something hit the door again, and it finally broke. It looked like it was made of paper as the dragons pulled the pieces apart, and Gideon sucked in a breath as he attempted to identify them. They weren't wearing clothing or armor that would tell him who these people were, but he couldn't see any of the symbols the Ogorth clan dragons and their allies had drawn on their bodies. They'd known they would have a hard time identifying the fighters, and it had felt like a good idea. It meant that Gideon knew that these people weren't friends.

He'd already suspected that much since they'd broken down the door, but he'd still had hope.

Just a tiny bit.

A dark orange dragon stepped forward and looked around the room. He couldn't miss Gideon, and when his gaze stopped on him, he grinned widely. It exposed his fangs, and while Gideon had never been afraid of a dragon, it still made him shiver.

They were going to eat him, weren't they?

"Look what I found," the dragon drawled. "A little human."

Gideon straightened his back, even though he *was* little next to most dragons. He was tempted to tell them who he was, but it sounded a little douchey — *do you know who I am* — and besides, he didn't want to give himself up as a hostage. It would be like the Saganto clan to do something to him just because of who he was and his role.

"I want to play with him," another dragon said behind the first one. This one was a muted green.

The orange dragon growled. "I saw him first."

God. They were going to tear Gideon apart because they couldn't decide who should have him. If there had been a window anywhere in the closet, Gideon would've thrown himself out of it. He'd rather die than have to deal with these dragons.

A loud shout in the room behind the dragons made them turn. The green one snarled and disappeared, but the orange one didn't follow. Instead, he moved toward Gideon, grabbing his arm and pulling him forward. He placed Gideon in front of his body, and Gideon was sure that he was a hostage now.

He realized that wasn't quite the case when they stepped into the bigger room. He wasn't just a hostage. He was a human shield, because the dragon was using him so the Ogorth clan dragons wouldn't attack him.

The asshole.

"Let me go, and I won't hurt him," the orange dragon said.

Gideon was pissed. He'd never been a fighter, but he'd taken a few self-defense lessons before coming here. His mother had insisted, and since it made her feel better, he'd gone along with it.

Thinking quickly, he raised a foot, then stomped onto one of the dragon's feet. The dragon yelped, and his hold on Gideon loosened, so Gideon turned around. He turned his hand so his palm was aimed toward the dragon's face, then hit the dragon's nose with it. Blood spurred from the wound, and the dragon reached for his face, slightly bending down.

That was when Gideon kneed him in the groin.

He hadn't been sure it would work on a dragon, but it did. The dragon squeaked and lowered his hands from his nose to his groin, cupping it like any human male would have. Gideon cocked his fist back, ready to hit the asshole on the nose again, but a hand caught his wrist. He tried jerking back, terrified that the dragon's friends were going to eat him, but the dragon holding his arm wasn't an enemy.

Gideon recognized the sign on the dragon's shoulder right away. He relaxed.

"I think you hurt him enough," the dragon said, sounding amused.

"I didn't mean to."

"Well, whether or not you meant it, you did a good thing."

Gideon agreed. He could never have killed anyone, and he hadn't expected to be able to beat up a dragon the way he had, but he was proud of himself. He hadn't been a victim. Even though he'd known he would never be able to win a fight with the dragon, he'd still stood up for himself, and he'd succeeded.

"The babies?" he asked.

"Everyone's safe. They locked themselves in another room, and we found them before you. They told us you were under attack." The guard looked around. "They didn't mention that you had everything in hand."

Gideon felt his cheeks heat. He didn't think the dragon was flirting or anything like that, mostly because the fact that he and Lisha were together was known around the palace. Ever since they'd started dating, gossip had run wild. Gideon didn't usually like gossip, but in this case, it had been useful because everyone knew he belonged to Lisha.

Someone cried out, and Gideon almost groaned. What was it now? He looked around, trying to find out what was happening, but he didn't see anything until the looked up.

Gideon did the same, and his eyes widened when he saw what was happening in the sky above the palace. Through the hole, he could see a group of four dragons carrying a struggling red dragon. That dragon was losing blood, but no one appeared to care. The red dragon was trying to get away, snapping at the legs of the dragons carrying them. One snapped back, and Gideon was sure they caught the red dragon's muzzle. The red dragon jerked away, making a wounded sound.

"Who is that?" he asked no one in particular.

He'd seen dragons being carried to the palace earlier in the fight, but they'd been wounded. They'd been happy to come back, but the red dragon seemed anything but. They were desperate to fly away, but the dragons carrying them weren't letting go.

Gideon was pretty sure he recognized one of them. He was still learning how to recognize dragons in their dragon forms, but there weren't many pitch-black dragons at the palace. That had to be Hogan, meaning that whoever he was carrying was important.

"I don't know, but I'm eager to find out," the guard said.

Gideon had no idea what was happening. He needed to check on the people he cared about, like Sheldon and the babies, and to find out what had happened to Lisha. No one in the palace would be able to tell him that because Lisha was outside, but maybe the four dragons flying to the landing pad had seen him. At the very least, if he ran up there, he'd be able to check in on Hogan. Cain would be happy to know that his partner was all right.

The problem was the running part. He wasn't far from the central stairs, but going up them was going to be a bitch. It would take ages, and he'd be out of breath by the time he reached the top.

"I can fly you up there," the guard said.

Gideon usually would say no because he didn't know this dragon, but there was no way he was staying away. "Please." The sooner he got to the landing pad, the sooner he could find out if Lisha was all right, and in the end, that was all that mattered.

CHAPTER FOURTEEN

Lisha knew something was happening when he heard people yelling. For a moment, he didn't understand what was going on, but Elodio, who had been following him since he'd saved him from the hunter, pointed a finger upward.

They were closer to the palace now, but still not close enough. Lisha's need to get there was urgent—he had to check in on Gideon—but the sight in front of him made him gape.

Four dragons were carrying a fifth dragon who was struggling to get away. Lisha was pretty sure he recognized Hogan, especially when the black dragon snapped at the red one.

"Who is that?" he asked, hoping someone around him would be able to answer.

"I'm pretty sure that's Sigmund."

It took Lisha a moment to realize what Elodio was saying. "The Saganto clan leader?"

Elodio was grinning like a fool. "Yeah. I saw him from afar earlier."

Lisha looked up again. Sigmund had been captured, and they were taking him back to the palace. Soon he'd be in the queen's hands, and she'd have control over him. "Who's supposed to take over the Saganto clan once Sigmund is gone?"

"His son should, but he's been wounded."

"Any second in command?"

Lisha remembered hearing something about the guy who'd represented the Saganto clan at the meeting of dragons. Bergen had fiercely opposed anything Queen Ita suggested, especially the alliance with the humans. He'd been an enemy from the beginning, and everyone knew it. There had been whispers since then that the Saganto clan was in league with the hunters, and it turned out they were.

And now, all of that was over. They'd captured Sigmund, and the ground around Lisha was covered in dead dragons and hunters.

Lisha needed to get to the palace.

He looked around, needing to make sure there were no wounded dragons who needed him. There were plenty of bodies, but most of the wounded had already been taken care of. Lisha should probably stay back, because he was the queen's healer, but there were others already working on the few people who still needed it. He could go home.

To Gideon.

He twisted his bag around his neck and shifted. Elodio didn't seem surprised and did the same, and together, they pushed off the ground and into the air. They had to navigate around the trees, but Lisha could spread his wings once they were above them. This time, he didn't pause to enjoy flying. He needed to get to the palace. He didn't even care about Sigmund. He just wanted to check on Gideon.

The room where Gideon and the others had been staying in wasn't in the spot where there was now a hole, but it was close by. They would have felt the explosion strongly, and it was too easy to imagine how freaked out everyone would have been. Lisha was also terrified because he'd seen enemy dragons getting in through the hole. What if they'd found the room? What if they'd hurt Gideon?

Lisha couldn't even think about that. Gideon might be under the rubble right at this moment, calling out for him, and he couldn't hear it. He couldn't do anything but fly toward the palace and pray his Gideon was all right.

Lisha was tempted to land in the hole, but Elodio guided

him toward the landing pad instead. Lisha snapped his teeth at him, but his new friend didn't seem to care. He clearly knew there were people important to Lisha in the palace, but he didn't want Lisha to do something stupid and hurt himself.

He wasn't wrong. If Lisha were to see one of the people he cared about wounded, or worse, he'd lose it. The clan still needed him, meaning he had to control himself. Besides, once he flew above the landing pad, he realized that most of the clan still in the palace seemed to have gathered here.

That wasn't surprising once he saw that Sigmund was right in the middle of the landing pad. The four dragons who'd carried him still surrounded him, each of them holding down one of his limbs. More dragons had trapped his wings, and the queen stood in front of him, staring him down. There were other captured dragons around the landing pad, all of them being restrained. They stared at their leader, and they had to know the war was over.

Even though the Saganto clan had terrorized the dragon world for so long, it was over. They'd lost, and soon everyone would know.

Lisha landed away from the queen and shifted, quickly looking around. He wanted to find out what was happening with Sigmund, but he needed Gideon more. He hoped Gideon was here, but when he couldn't see him, he started freaking out again.

Until something slammed against his side.

Lisha stumbled, thankful that Elodio was still by his other side because he kept him upright. Lisha's arms went around the person who'd slammed against him by instinct, and he was glad to have followed that instinct when he realized it was Gideon.

He buried his face against Gideon's hair and inhaled. When he let go of the breath, his shoulders slumped in relief, and he allowed himself to believe everything would be all right.

The war was over, and Gideon was in Lisha's arms. Everything was perfect.

"Are you okay?" he asked Gideon as he pushed him back to look at him. He needed to make sure Gideon wasn't hurt, that he hadn't been caught in the explosion.

Gideon was pale, but he seemed to be all right, even though his clothes were rumpled. His glasses were slightly crooked on his nose, and Lisha straightened them, loving how it made Gideon blush.

"I'm fine. What about you?"

Lisha grinned and kissed Gideon. It seemed to be answer enough because Gideon clung to him, making Lisha wonder if he was trying to make them one entity. He seemed to want to climb into Lisha and never leave, and if he could find a way to make that work, Lisha would be on board.

"Everyone is all right," Gideon said as they separated. "The babies are fine, and so is everyone else. I saw most of our friends fly back in, including Hogan."

Lisha turned toward Hogan, who was still at the center of the landing pad. Everyone around it was whispering, waiting to see what the queen would do.

Lisha was, too. The war was over, but they needed everyone in the Saganto clan to be aware of that. They needed everyone in the dragon world to be aware of it. They had to know that if anyone attacked the Ogorth clan, they would face their wrath and lose.

The Ogorth clan had faced their most dangerous enemy and won. The victory was theirs, and even though Lisha would need time to deal with everything that had happened today, he allowed relief to take over.

Soon enough, he'd have to face the horror of the war. He already had, but he was nowhere near done. For a few moments, though, he could bask in the knowledge that all of it was over.

Gideon was never letting Lisha go. He'd been so sure something had happened to him that he'd almost cried in relief when he'd seen him landing. Lisha hadn't heard him because of how many people were on the landing pad, and Gideon would never forget how panicked he'd looked. Gideon had made his way through the crowd, and they were finally reunited.

They'd both survived. They were both all right, at least physically. Gideon had no doubt that they'd have to deal with the aftermath of the war soon, but for now, they could allow themselves to feel relief.

It was time to end this. The queen had been silent, but Gideon knew it wouldn't be forever. She had the Saganto clan leader in front of her, trussed up like a sausage. The dragons keeping him on the ground seemed more than happy to do so. Gideon could see Hogan grinning like a loon, even from a distance.

Thankfully, everyone around Gideon and Lisha wanted to hear what was happening, so the landing pad was eerily quiet. They were all waiting to see what the queen would do, and Gideon knew they wouldn't be disappointed.

"The war is over," the queen declared, her voice loud over the silence.

The Saganto clan leader roared. Gideon felt safe, but that was because he was surrounded by dragons. If he hadn't been, he would have run away.

"Shift back, Sigmund," the queen ordered. "If you want to explain yourself, this is your only opportunity. Your people already know you've been captured. They're fleeing, and they won't come back for you."

Gideon didn't expect Sigmund to shift, so he was surprised

when he did. The people keeping him down moved quickly so he wouldn't be able to run away, and Hogan was still grinning when he grabbed one of Sigmund's arms. Gideon didn't think he'd seen him smile so much since he'd met him. Hogan was usually a serious, almost grim kind of person, and it was a little creepy to see him like this.

Sigmund was bleeding, and now that he was in his human form, Gideon could see it came from his thigh. Even from a distance, Gideon could see the wound was bad, and while he didn't feel sorry for Sigmund, he had to look away because his stomach churned at the sight of the torn flesh.

Sigmund remained silent.

Gideon half expected him to start ranting, but it was clear that he and his people had lost and that they'd been on the wrong side of this fight.

Sigmund stared at the queen, and luckily, looks couldn't kill.

She stared back, her expression more serene, but then, she'd won. "Your son is wounded and ran," she said. "Bergen is dead. The same goes for most of the army you amassed, and those who aren't dead or wounded are fleeing. You don't have anyone left. You don't have *anything* left."

"You might think you've won, but there will be others. My son will take over as soon as he's better," Sigmund said.

Maybe he was right, and others would try to do what he'd done, but Gideon doubted they would succeed. Sigmund had done all of this because he'd had his entire clan behind him, willing or not. Now, his clan was decimated. There were some members still alive, but they'd fled, and even if Sigmund's son managed to pull them back together, there still wouldn't be more than a handful of dragons. Gideon didn't have exact numbers, but most of Sigmund's clan was dead. The people he'd left behind weren't, but how many were there? Gideon was sure the queen had already sent someone to deal with them. They would be mostly older dragons and children, and while Gideon had no idea what would happen to them, he trusted the queen to be fair.

Something Sigmund hadn't been, and now, he'd pay for it.

"Surrender," the queen ordered.

"Never," Sigmund snarled.

The queen nodded as if she wasn't surprised. Gideon expected her to order Sigmund to be killed, but instead, she gestured at the dragons holding him to take him away.

"I will meet with the other clan leaders, and together, we'll decide what to do with you," she told Sigmund. "Don't expect us to feel sorry for you or to have mercy. After all the clans you've destroyed, the only outcome will be death."

Gideon shivered. His superiors would probably try to get him to convince the queen and the other leaders not to do that, but he wouldn't. Sigmund was their prisoner, and this was a dragon problem. They would decide how to solve it, and the human government had nothing to do with it. Besides, even though Gideon despised Sigmund, he wouldn't wish for anyone to become an experiment or whatever the government had in mind for him. Gideon didn't know for sure, and he wasn't planning to find out. It wasn't his place.

Everyone continued to be silent as Sigmund struggled against the dragons taking him away. He could barely put weight on his leg, so they had to carry him. Gideon was pretty sure they'd be tempted to throw him down the stairs rather than carry him all the way down, especially if Hogan was the one making decisions.

He didn't have an opportunity to find out. As soon as Sigmund was out of sight, whispers started in the crowd. The queen raised her hands, and silence fell again.

"The war is over," she announced. "We've all lost people. We're all in pain. Unfortunately, even though the fight is over, our work isn't. We need to gather and honor our dead and help our wounded and the dragons hurt by the Saganto clan. But tonight, we can relax. We can celebrate. We might have lost many dragons, but they knew what they were fighting for, and we should honor them. We won, and so have they, even though they're not here to see it."

Gideon's chest felt tight. He didn't know who they'd lost, but they'd find out before the end of the day. There would be tears and pain, but everyone who had died knew what they were fighting for. They'd known it was a possibility, and they'd sacrificed themselves anyway. It didn't help dull the pain, but that wasn't what they should focus on, at least not today.

Today was for celebrations. Today was for the living.

And tomorrow would be for grief.

Lisha's day was far from over. Now that the Saganto clan was gone, he should go to the infirmary and work even harder than he had this morning. There were dozens of wounded, and that was only counting the Ogorth clan and their allies. There would be even more wounded Saganto clan members, and Lisha had every intention of helping them, too. He didn't know what would happen to them after that, but even if they died, he would feel like he'd done his job.

"How is everyone?" he asked, turning to Gideon.

"They're fine. Christian was hurt when he fell while they were running, but I was told it was just a broken arm. He'll be okay."

"The others?"

"Everyone who was with me is all right. We saw Hogan, but the other dragons are still out there."

Lisha nodded. He looked at the crowd, trying to find their friends. Now that the queen was done talking, he wasn't surprised to see Morven quickly move toward her. He was followed by most of his team and Orran, who'd been with the queen and the other leaders in the throne room. Hogan was the only one who wasn't here, but that was because he was still dragging Sigmund to the cells.

Lisha felt a bit better, even though he could see that Octavia was limping. Slavin had a long gash on his arm, while Dray's head had been bandaged. But they were all here, and they were all on their feet. That had to mean they would be all right.

Lisha wouldn't have it any other way.

His people had survived, and he'd make sure they were fine, be it the last thing he did. It made him feel slightly guilty because, as a healer, he shouldn't play favorites, but these people were his priority. Once he'd checked them over, he could return to the infirmary and care for everyone else.

"I know what you're thinking," Gideon drawled.

Lisha wasn't surprised. "Do you?"

"I don't know if they'll allow you to fuss over them. They're going to be busy for the rest of the day and probably the rest of the week."

Lisha tightened his jaw. "I don't care how busy they are. If they're wounded, I'm going to take care of them."

Gideon beamed. "And that's why we love you."

Emotion gripped Lisha's throat. "I love you, too," he murmured.

He'd been so close to never being able to say that to Gideon again. The thought made him want to cry, and he reminded himself that they'd made it. They were fine, and now the war was over, that wasn't going to change.

Gideon hooked an arm around Lisha's waist and pulled him closer. For a moment, they stayed wrapped around each other. Lisha knew he needed to get to work, but he found himself unable to move. He already knew Gideon was fine, but reassuring himself would take more than five minutes. He'd probably have nightmares, especially after seeing how close Gideon had been to the explosion that had taken down part of the palace.

"We did it," Gideon whispered. "The Ogorth clan won, and the Saganto clan is a thing of the past."

Lisha snorted. "Not yet."

Gideon nodded. "Not yet," he agreed. "But soon, they will be, and once they are, we can start building our life together."

Lisha couldn't wait. "What will you be doing for the rest of the day?"

He had a hard time letting go of Gideon, but he had to. Lisha needed to focus on his patients, and there was no doubt Gideon had to contact his superiors and talk to the queen and their allies. Everyone would be busy, but tonight, they could finally go to sleep knowing they wouldn't be attacked during the night and that tomorrow, when they woke up, they would be at peace.

"I'm sure my superiors have already heard that we won the war, but they'll still want me to call them. I have to talk to the leaders of the human teams who fought against the hunters and see what happened there and let the queen know. You'll be in the infirmary?"

"For the rest of the day and probably part of the night."

"I know how important healing people is to you, but you're already exhausted. I'm not going to tell you not to do anything else today because I know you wouldn't listen to me but don't push yourself too hard. You won't be any use to anyone if you fall on your face because you're so tired that you can't think straight. Don't make mistakes you could regret."

Lisha was glad that Gideon wasn't trying to force him to change his mind, but he was right. Lisha risked hurting someone if he got too tired. That was the last thing he wanted, but it would be hard to resist the urge to continue working until he'd seen every dragon and human who needed him.

That was why he needed Gideon. He had no doubt that Gideon would come and find him in the infirmary later today. He'd make sure Lisha had lunch, and once dinner came, he'd force Lisha to take a break. They could finally get a good night's sleep.

The horror of the war was still there, but Lisha found himself relaxing. He needed to get to work, but he leaned against Gideon and breathed.

That moment didn't last long enough. Someone touched Lisha's arm, and when he turned, his work started. One of the nurses needed his help in the infirmary tent they'd set up on the landing pad. After one last kiss to Gideon, Lisha rushed there, ready to help.

That was what he did for the rest of the day. He stayed in the infirmary on the landing pad long enough to make sure everyone who was there was stable. They couldn't do much on the landing pad because it wasn't set up as a real infirmary, so everyone who was badly wounded was eventually sent down. There were too many people, and the infirmary was crowded, so they only kept the most severe cases there. It took a while to triage everyone and even longer to help them.

Lisha focused on the worst cases, along with the other experienced healers and doctors. The infirmary smelled of blood and death, but Lisha pushed past it.

He was already exhausted by the time Gideon forced him to take half an hour off for lunch. He was even more exhausted when night fell and Gideon came to get him, declaring his day was over.

"I still have people to help," Lisha argued.

"I know. You'll have people to help for days, if not weeks. You're not the only healer here, though. Some of them took the afternoon off, and they'll take your place and care for the wounded overnight."

Gideon's tone was uncompromising. Lisha found himself

tempted to tell him to leave, but he pressed his lips together. He was exhausted and needed to attend the celebration dinner tonight. He was pretty sure he'd end up falling asleep with his face on his plate, but even if he did, Gideon would take care of him.

That was one thing he was sure of. Gideon would always take care of him, even when he didn't take care of himself. It wouldn't be easy to stop overworking himself like he used to do before, but he needed to make an effort. It wasn't just him anymore. Now, it was him and Gideon, and they had their entire future together.

EPILOGUE

Lisha didn't think he'd ever been so tired. He felt like he'd been working for weeks rather than days, and even though Gideon made sure he got enough sleep and food, it didn't feel like enough. Lisha felt that he was going to break, and he was sure he wasn't the only one.

One of the nurses *had* broken. He'd started crying a few hours earlier, and Lisha had sent him home. No one had yet had the time or space they needed to deal with the war and what they'd seen, and they were all working on too-little sleep and trying to ignore their nightmares. Eventually, things would slow down enough that they couldn't ignore them anymore, and Lisha wasn't looking forward to that.

He leaned against the infirmary wall, sucking in a breath, then another. He had just finished dealing with a patient, and while another was already waiting for him, he needed a few seconds of respite.

Everyone was in the same boat. All the healers and nurses were working most of the time. There weren't as many emergencies as before, but a lot of the dragons had wounds that would take a while to recover from. Even though everyone was stabilized, Lisha still had to check in on every single patient every day, but thankfully, he wasn't working alone.

But the infirmary was emptying. Most clan leaders had taken their dragons back to their homes if they could be moved. Not everyone could, and those who were still here were Lisha's responsibility.

He wasn't the only one working so hard. Everyone was in

different roles. Gideon was running around, talking to his people and the queen, making sure everyone was on the same page. From what he'd told Lisha, the government hadn't been happy that the queen had executed Sigmund without talking to them first. Lisha didn't understand why they thought she might have. They weren't dragons, and while they were allies, this was a decision she and the other dragon leaders had taken.

No one had been surprised when Sigmund had been executed. It was what he'd deserved, and while Lisha usually mourned the loss of life, in this case, he couldn't. The world was a better place without Sigmund, and no one could ever convince him otherwise.

The Saganto clan wasn't entirely gone. As many survivors as possible had been captured, but without knowing what they'd done and why they'd done it, it wasn't easy to make decisions about their future. Luckily, the queen didn't have to do so on her own, but it was still a mess, especially with the survivors who'd remained at the Saganto clan's home.

There weren't many of them. Most were children and elder dragons, along with a few guards, and they'd surrendered right away. The queen and the others were still making decisions on what would be done with them, but those people hadn't done anything in the war. They couldn't be allowed to keep living there, but they wouldn't be killed, either.

Lisha didn't know for sure what the queen would decide, but he was ready to bet she'd divide them up among the remaining clans. It wasn't usually done beyond people moving from one clan to another because they wanted to be with a partner, but maybe it was time for the dragons to stop isolating themselves. They'd been so afraid to start another war that they'd refused to spend any length of time together, but a war had started anyway. They needed to find a way to live together, and hopefully, that would be one result of the war.

"Can you believe he told us we were welcomed to become clan members?" Lisha heard a human doctor whisper to one of the human guards.

He made sure to act as if he wasn't listening to them, but he was curious.

Like most of the people here, he'd been at the celebration dinner the day the war had ended. Most dragons had given the humans a wide berth, and it had hurt a bit to see, even though it was understandable. Everyone had been stunned when Killian, the Eiloren king, declared that anyone who had helped win the war, human or dragon, had a place with the Eiloren clan. He was trying extremely hard to change things, and while Lisha didn't know if this was the right way to do so, at least he was trying.

"What do you think of the offer?" the soldier asked.

"I don't know."

"You sound tempted. You're not thinking about it, are you?"

Lisha peeked at the doctor. The last few days had been a whirlwind of too many things for him to be able to remember the man's name, but he'd worked with him several times. The doctor was a good man and a good healer, and Lisha had been glad to have him by his side. He'd learned a lot when it came to healing humans, and he was sure the doctor had learned just as much when it came to healing dragons.

"Maybe," the doctor said. "Think about it. Do you know how much I could learn by living with them?"

"You'd have to leave everything behind."

The doctor shrugged. "That's fine. I don't have a lot, anyway."

"You have me," the soldier pointed out.

Lisha squinted, trying to understand what they were to each other. The soldier didn't sound angry, but rather, sad and confused. They weren't touching in the way two people in love would, but what did Lisha know? He didn't have that much experience when it came to relationships.

"I do, and I love you, but I want to do this."

"I'm not going to try to change your mind, but you need to think about it before you do anything."

The doctor grinned. "I always do."

It sounded like he'd already made his decision. Lisha waited until Taylor, the soldier, left the infirmary to turn to the doctor. Now that he was close enough, he could see the doctor's name on his white coat, and it jogged his memory.

"Hey, Palmer," he said.

Palmer smiled. "Heard that, didn't you?"

"I wasn't spying on you."

"I never said you were."

"Your . . . Taylor didn't sound happy that you're thinking of moving."

"That's because my brother worries too much. I'll be fine, though. I can't wait. It was great to stay with the Ogorth clan, but I know it's not permanent, you know? Maybe moving in with the Eiloren clan will be even better."

"I'm sure they'll need healers and doctors, so they won't say no."

"I just want to help, and they have wounded warriors, too. They need someone, and while I'm sure they have healers, another pair of hands will be useful."

"Seeing so many humans is odd, but it's also good."

Palmer nodded. "We're learning to live together."

And now that the Saganto clan was gone, there would be no war between dragons and humans. Lisha didn't fool himself into thinking everything would be smooth and without problems, but they could deal with it. It would take time and effort, but Lisha truly believed they could find a way to make it work.

They had to, because he wasn't giving up on Gideon.

If Gideon heard the word *execution* one more time, he'd scream. In fact, he was so tempted to do so now that he had to press his lips together hard to resist.

"I'm sorry you're disappointed, but it wasn't our decision to make," he said. "He's been executed, and his body was burned, along with the bodies of his dragons."

"What about the survivors?"

Luckily, this was a conference call, not a video call. It meant that whoever the asshole was asking Gideon couldn't see him scowl.

Gideon had been on so many calls with so many people he didn't know these past few days that he'd lost track of the names. He didn't need to remember them, anyway. For most, calling them Asshole One, Asshole Two, and so on was okay.

If he remembered correctly, this was Asshole Twelve.

"They've already been divided between the remaining clans," he explained. "No one is going to hand them over to humans."

"I don't expect them to. I was just wondering if some of them might want to move to the human world."

"I think at the moment, everyone is focused on healing and setting things right here." And if any dragon was tempted to move to the human world, Gideon would try to change their mind.

He might be human, but he wasn't blind to how cruel some humans were, especially some of those who were part of the government. They saw dragons as a novelty they needed to examine and experiment on, and Gideon couldn't allow that to happen. He wouldn't be able to stop every dragon, but he could do his best to ensure they knew what would wait for them if they decided to take Asshole Twelve's offer.

A quick knock on the door made Gideon look up. He didn't

care who it was as long as they gave him an excuse to end this meeting. "I apologize, but I have another meeting," he said. "I'm sure we can talk later."

"You can't hang up like this," Asshole Twelve protested.

"One of the queen's advisors is here," Gideon lied.

The door opened, and Lisha peeked in. He wasn't one of the queen's advisors, but that was fine. Gideon wanted to see him even more.

"Fine," Asshole Twelve muttered. "But think about what I said and try to convince at least a few of them."

"Of course."

Gideon jabbed his finger on his phone, desperately needing to hang up. Once he had, he checked to be sure, then he turned his chair and opened his arms.

He didn't have to say anything. Lisha scrambled into his lap and burrowed against him, pressing his head under Gideon's chin. He had to arch his back to do so, so he wouldn't stay in this position for long, but he could take a few seconds to relax and rest.

"What do you have to convince people of?" Lisha muttered.

"That they want to move into the human world."

Lisha snorted. "Why would anyone want that?"

"I can't exactly tell my superiors that, but I don't think anyone would want that. If they did, I'd try to change their mind."

It would take a long time for humans to truly accept dragons. In the meantime, it would be better for dragons to stay with their clans. Hopefully, everyone would understand that, including the younger dragons. Gideon understood they might be tempted, but he'd fight in order to keep them safe.

It was an odd position to be in. He was human, and he should be on the government's side. Instead, he was firmly on the dragons' side. He wouldn't let anyone take advantage of them or hurt them, and that was that.

"I'm tired," Lisha mumbled.

Gideon wrapped his arms around him. "Then rest for a bit. I'll wake you up in half an hour."

Lisha nodded and pressed closer. Gideon couldn't look away from him, so he watched him as he fell asleep almost instantly.

The war might be over, but they were still dealing with the aftermath. That would take a while, and not everyone would fully recover, but at least now they didn't have to be afraid anymore. The Saganto clan was gone, and no matter how long it took, everyone could finally start living again.

Including Lisha and Gideon.

ABOUT THE AUTHOR

Catherine is the creator of several series, most of them paranormal, including the Whitedell Pride Series and the Gillham Pack Series. While she graduated in translation, she decided to go the writer's way because it was more fun to create her own stories and characters.

She's been living in Italy for more than twenty years, but she's a daughter of the North — Belgium to be precise — and she misses it so much that she's already planning to move back.

She loves pizza — probably too much — her son, her pets, and of course, books. She sneaks some reading time into her schedule every time she has five minutes free from writing, demands from her various pets and son, and lastly, housework.

Connect with her:

lievens.catherine@gmail.com
BookBub: https://www.bookbub.com/authors/catherine-lievens
Website: https://authorcatherinelievens.com/
Facebook: https://www.facebook.com/catherine.lievens.9
Facebook Group: https://www.facebook.com/groups/411788002341528/
Twitter: https://twitter.com/authorCLievens
Newsletter: http://eepurl.com/c-uvKn

www.ingramcontent.com/pod-product-compliance
Lightning Source LLC
Chambersburg PA
CBHW060820120626
46557CB00001B/298